STARFLEET ACADEMY

THE EDGE

by Rudy Josephs

Simon Spotlight
New York London Toronto Sydney

Contents

CH.1.28
Survival Course

Starfleet Academy, Week One

Plebeians.

It was what they called the commoners in ancient Rome. The lower class.

In the year 2255 the word had generally slipped out of usage on Earth. The lower class no longer existed. Not in terms of monetary wealth. Everyone was equal.

Mostly.

Plebeians still existed on the campus of Starfleet Academy in San Francisco. Plebes were considered the lowest of the low. They were the first-year cadets who had yet to prove themselves. These incoming students could shine like a supernova or fade like a white dwarf.

There was nothing common about Cadet James T. Kirk as he stood in the center of the pack of first-year cadets. They may have been more than five hundred kilometers from the Academy campus, but that much was clear. If not to Kirk, then to everyone around him.

Eyes shifted in Kirk's direction. Whispers carried his name across the arid Mojave Desert. Jim Kirk was used to being noticed back home in Iowa. Local law enforcement kept pretty good tabs on him, along with the fathers of one or two of his ex-girlfriends. Being the town screwup came with its fair amount of sideways glances and whispered conversations. He'd been through it before. But that didn't explain why he was getting the same treatment from a bunch of strangers.

Kirk returned the stares in defiance, sizing up the competition. Dozens of first years took positions along the starting line around him. These would be his friends and, more than likely, *enemies* over the next four years at Starfleet Academy.

Three years, Kirk corrected himself. He'd promised Captain Pike that he would graduate in three years. Bragged about it, actually. It wasn't the first rash promise he'd made in his life. Probably wouldn't be the last.

Starfleet Academy accepted the best and the brightest members of the United Federation of Planets to prepare them for life among the stars. Most of the students around him were human, but there were representatives from a number of alien races from Andorians to Zaranites. It was easy to be anonymous in a sea of students that came in all sizes, shapes, and colors in the spectrum.

Yet there was another reason he was so surprised that many of his classmates seemed to be focused on him. The green guy beside him, for instance, couldn't take his eyes off Kirk.

"Problem?" Kirk asked. The guy shrugged and moved off, but Kirk wasn't done with him. "Something on my face?"

It was a joke, but Kirk was starting to think he had a zit the size of Jupiter or something equally disfiguring going on. He couldn't possibly be the most interesting person around. Why was he getting such attention?

"They're looking for your halo," a voice behind him said.

Kirk turned to see a girl raising her arms up to the bright sky, stretching her muscles before the race. She was human, with long, dark hair; copper-toned skin; and piercing green eyes.

"What?" he asked.

Her muscular legs strained against the fabric of her uniform pants as she stretched her left leg in front of her right. The traditional skirts worn by the female cadets had been exchanged for the more appropriate uniform pants for the terrain. "You know, halos? Angels wear them? Sons of angels, too, I hear." She switched position, placing her right leg in front. "How does it feel to be famous already?"

"Feels like crap," Kirk said.

"Cheeky. I like that." She gave a curt nod of her head

and a brief smile. "Monica Lynne."

"Jim Kirk," he said out of reflex. She clearly knew who he was. He guessed everyone did. It shouldn't have been a surprise.

Jim's dad, George Kirk, had died saving his wife, newborn son, and eight hundred members of the crew of the USS *Kelvin*. Captain Pike had needlessly reminded Kirk of that fact as a way of convincing him to enlist at Starfleet Academy. Word must have spread.

Kirk joined Lynne in her stretching routine. He hadn't been taking this race seriously, but it didn't hurt to be prepared for whatever they were about to endure. It also gave him a reason to move a little closer to her.

The desert sun beat down on his back as he bent beside Lynne. This was one of the biggest tests he'd have to endure in his first year at Starfleet Academy—but for unorthodox reasons. The cadets weren't getting graded; no professors were present. The Starfleet Academy Desert Survival Course wasn't even listed as part of the curriculum. In spite of all that, Kirk had already been warned that there was only one test at Starfleet Academy that was more important to his career. He wouldn't take that until senior year.

The winner of the survival course would be known to all as the leader of the pack of first-year cadets. Ahead of his peers before the first class was called into session. Upperclassmen would treat that plebe with a respect not afforded the other first-year students. Word would get back to the professors, who would know to keep an eye out for that one. The survival course had only one winner. Everyone else came in last.

Normally, Kirk wouldn't have cared. He didn't need a silly race to prove anything. But this was Kirk's first chance to make a name for himself separate from his father's. The father he had never even met.

Life didn't provide opportunities like that too often.

•   ·   ✦   ✦   •   ✦   ·•·

Several meters ahead of Kirk, Cadet Nyota Uhura finished her stretching routine and stepped up to the starting line. People were already jostling for position, wanting to be the first off the line. She pushed back, unwilling to give up her spot.

Other cadets had wasted time disembarking the shuttles asking pointless questions about why their communicators were being taken away. Why they couldn't bring any tricorders with them to survey the landscape or phasers to protect themselves from whatever dangers might be out there.

Uhura had quietly handed everything over and hurried to the starting line to claim her space. She needed nothing but her body and her wits to get her through the course.

The people standing at the front with her would be her main competition while she was at the Academy. Most of the people she'd met on her first trip to the Academy were already lost in the crowd. Not surprising. The kind of guys who would get in a random bar fight while in uniform were not the cadets she wanted to associate with. That was one of the reasons she was glad she continually passed up the not-so-subtle flirtations from Jim Kirk.

She'd already seen Kirk in the pack not that far behind her. He hadn't caught her noticing him, which was good. The last thing she needed was for him to think she was interested. She wasn't.

Neither was he, it seemed. Kirk was already chatting up someone else.

Good. She didn't have time for unwelcome attention. She was at the Academy for one purpose. If only someone would explain that to the Andorian beside her.

The two antennae peeking out from the white hair on his pale blue head turned in her direction. He was stretching his legs in a manner that he probably thought looked enticing.

It didn't.

Thanas had introduced himself to her on the shuttle ride from the Academy to the desert and hadn't left her alone since. "You should stick with me in the race. We'd make a good team."

Considering he knew practically nothing about her, it wasn't hard to see through the thinly veiled come on. "This isn't a team competition."

"Nothing wrong with coming in second."

She held a hand over her eyes, blocking out the sun while she took in the terrain in a blatant attempt to ignore him. "Then I'm glad you won't mind."

She wasn't even sure where the finish line was. The cadets had been pointed in a westerly direction and told to run toward the setting sun until they reached the end. Except no end was visible to the naked eye. Just miles and miles of empty desert.

Correction. Not *empty*. It was filled with natural, and probably unnatural, obstacles. If they'd wanted a flat-out race, they could have used the track at the Academy or set them loose on the streets of San Francisco. The desert had been chosen for a reason. They wanted a race on unfamiliar ground.

Most of the cadets lived in modern cities with all the amenities: moving sidewalks, turbo lifts, and even transporters to get them around. Oh, they were all fit. They trained in gyms and on sports fields. Under controlled conditions.

Only a few of them were probably used to racing on this kind of terrain. That was one thing Uhura had going for her. Growing up in her native Africa, Uhura had some experience with this type of climate. She might not be able to compete with a cadet that had grown up on the desert planet of Vulcan, but she could hold her own.

Thanas gave up on his useless warm-up exercises when

he realized she'd stopped paying him any attention. He was posing more than stretching, anyway. Some of the girls around them were watching. They could have him. Uhura was only interested in beating him.

Him and everyone else.

A group of upperclassmen had gathered on a rock formation to the side of the starting line, standing a dozen feet above the heads of the cadets. A visual representation that they thought they were above the plebes. The expressions on their faces ranged from smug superiority to mounting concern. Probably remembering back to their performance on the same race.

Uhura wondered if she'd be standing on that rock in a few years. Would she make it through to graduation? Would she make it through this race?

Her face set with determination. Of course she would. But she couldn't imagine coming back here to be a spectator for the intimidation of first-year cadets. That was a part of the Academy experience she had no interest in embracing.

One of the upperclassmen, who had been on Uhura's shuttle, sprang up to the topmost point of the large boulder his cohorts had collected on. His cocky stance left no doubt in Uhura's mind that he was the cadet who won the race in his freshman year. It was probably his duty to get the race started.

A smile came to her lips as she reconsidered coming back in her senior year. She would if she were the winner.

Thanas leaned forward beside her. "Here we go."

She mirrored his stance, preparing to leap off the starting line the moment the race began.

The upperclassman raised his communicator to his mouth. His voice was projected to speakers that surrounded the cadets. "Good morning, plebes. What stands before you is the Starfleet Academy Desert Survival Course."

Behind Uhura, the rest of the cadets fell into a ready stance.

"Your mission is to be the first to get to the end," he continued. "That's it. There are no rules. No other objectives. And no second place. You'll get no prize for winning. No grade. No commendation. Nothing but the knowledge that you are the best of the best among your peers."

The sun glinted off the phaser he raised. "The race will start on my mark."

A bolt of phaser fire shot into the air.

CH.2.28
Teammates

Kirk muscled past the cadets who were too slow off the block, powering to the front of the pack. He'd already set his sights on the guy he'd identified as his main competition, a big blue Andorian who was the first one off the line.

Out of the corner of his eye, Kirk realized he'd blown past Cadet Uhura. No first name given. He didn't slow to exchange pleasantries. He kept moving forward, pretty sure he heard her say "Idiot" as he passed her and the Andorian.

A hand grabbed Kirk's uniform collar, pulling him backward. He struggled against the grip, unable to believe that another cadet would so blatantly cheat, even though they had been told the race had no rules. He figured it was the Andorian and swung a punch to break free.

Lynne stopped his fist before it connected. Her grip was formidable.

"What the—"

"Nice way to thank a person," she said as other racers blew past them.

"Thank you? For holding me up? Let go."

She released her iron grasp. "It's your funeral. This race is a marathon, not a sprint."

Kirk was about to ask her what she meant when he saw the Andorian drop back to let a line of cadets pass before they disappeared in a dirt cloud. The mass of racers around them slowed to a near halt as the dust cleared.

"It's also booby-trapped," Lynne added unnecessarily. "Let the ones who run blindly find all the traps for us."

Kirk grunted a reluctant thanks. He didn't really want to hold back. The only way he was going to show these other cadets what he could do was by attacking the race full force. But Lynne had saved him from that ill-advised plan. A half-dozen of their peers were pulling themselves out of a pit for making the same mistake he'd been about to make.

Lynne hurdled over the ditch. Most of the racers chose to run around the trap. The trench had been dug out for more than two dozen meters. The route added countless seconds to the race. Seconds that could make all the difference in the end.

Kirk bound through the air, landing beside her. He wanted to say something flirty, but she took off running as soon as he hit the ground, already making her way to the front of the racers. It was probably smart to stick with

Lynne. She'd already proven herself a valuable teammate.

Although this had little to do with his true motivation for wanting to be near her.

He was immediately rewarded for this decision when she threw an arm out to stop him from stepping on a stun-mine buried under the dirt. It took out another racer who dropped to the ground unconscious.

"Thanks."

"Pick it up, Kirk," Lynne said with a smile. "Having to keep saving your butt is slowing me down."

Kirk tackled Lynne to the ground as a blast of phaser fire cut through the air in the space where she had been standing.

He spit out a mouthful of dirt. "You were saying?"

"By my count, you still owe me one." Lynne wiped the dirt from her face, spitting a fair amount of it out as well. "You can get off me now."

"Just want to make sure another one of those phaser blasts isn't coming along."

Lynne's body shook with laughter beneath him. He was tempted to roll her over and kiss her right there. It would have been sudden and unexpected, and maybe a little unwelcome. But this strange girl seemed to like that kind of impetuousness as much as he did.

The moment passed. Kirk got off the ground, holding a hand out to assist her. She smacked it away lightly and sprang to her feet on her own, taking off without a word. He followed. Sticking with her was definitely making the race more enjoyable.

The desert terrain grew rougher with every step. Rocks and shrubs now filled the area that had started out as flat, packed soil. There was no clear path to follow. All Kirk could do was follow in the steps of the cadets in front of him, keeping an eye out for traps or wildlife.

A cadet went down—hard—several meters in front of Kirk. Another cadet stopped to help him, then jumped back. Kirk thought he heard the word "snake" as he approached. He altered his route out of caution.

An emergency flare shot into the sky. It was the one thing the cadets had been handed when they left the shuttles. The downed cadet was transported away, disappearing in a swirling mist of light. A medical student would tend to the wound. If it was snakebite, there would surely be antivenom in one of the shuttles.

Kirk's thoughts turned to his one real friend, Leonard McCoy. He'd taken to calling him Bones after a joke the guy had made when they met. And Bones hadn't been in anywhere at the starting line. Kirk had looked. *Why wasn't he in the race?*

It was a pointless question for the moment. He had to focus on the terrain ahead of him. Kirk was not about to let a little snake take him out.

Three miles into the race, the traps weren't as much of a concern as the fatigue setting in. Cadets that hadn't anticipated the length of the race were slowing, like Lynne had foretold. Kirk would have fallen back like the rest of them if he hadn't listened to her. They kept a steady pace together—not too fast, not too slow.

A young kid Kirk met on the shuttle fell into step with them. They nodded hello. Kirk couldn't remember his name, but he did recall that the kid hailed from the lunar colony. That might have explained the deep huffing breaths he took as he struggled to stay on his feet. From what Kirk had heard, people who grew up in one of the colonies on the moon tended to have a hard time fighting Earth's gravity.

The Andorian first off the line had slowed his pace as well. Whether that was part of his race strategy or he was keeping stride with Uhura was unclear to Kirk. Probably a bit of both. He seemed to be flirting with her the whole time. At least, that's what Kirk assumed. He doubted they were exchanging recipes. By the exasperated look on her face, Kirk figured the Andorian was doing about as well with her as *he* had.

Uhura sidestepped some kind of trigger device that sent a barrage of dirt into the Andorian's face. It didn't slow him any, but it was entertaining to watch.

"Friend of yours?" Lynne asked with a slight smirk when she caught him staring.

"Acquaintance."

"Doesn't seem like your type," she said.

"She could be. How would you know?" Kirk asked.

"I meant the blue guy." She picked up her pace, pulling ahead of him.

Kirk sent a smile and a shrug in the direction of the kid from the lunar colony before taking off after her.

A few long sprints and Kirk was once again beside Lynne. A couple strides more and he finally passed her. A moment later he felt her tugging on his collar. This time, he recognized it as a warning. Up ahead, several of the cadets had stopped. It didn't take him long to figure out why.

The course had taken them to a cliff. The desert continued off in the distance, but it was much closer to sea level.

Kirk and Lynne slowed, but didn't stop until they reached the edge. The cliff ran on for about a half mile in either direction. The left side of the cliff eventually dipped into a shallow hill that would carry them safely to the bottom. Some cadets were already running in that direction, even though it would add minutes to the race.

Lynne didn't hesitate to join the cadets taking the direct path down the cliff's face. Kirk was right alongside her. He dropped to the ground and went over the side, finding the hand- and footholds the cadets before him had taken.

The last time Kirk had gone over the edge of a cliff, he'd sent a vintage Chevrolet Sting Ray careening to the bottom, nearly taking him along for the ride. He was still just a boy then. He was older now, but not necessarily wiser. He maintained a steady pace as he descended the cliff, slow enough to keep him from falling, but fast enough to keep him ahead of the pack.

The kid from the lunar colony wasn't as patient.

He zipped toward them, heading to the bottom at a dangerous rate. The kid had impressive climbing skills, which Kirk suspected had come from zero-g rock climbing on the moon. A fall from this height would hurt a lot more with Earth's gravity than it did on the moon.

Rocks and debris came showering down on them as the kid made his progress.

"Watch it!" Kirk warned. He and Lynne were halfway to the bottom. They didn't need a stray rock taking them out of the competition.

"Sorry," the kid called back without slowing. Kirk kept his head down as more dirt landed on him.

He was about to shout another warning when the kid lost his grip, falling away from the rock face. Kirk reached his arm across Lynne's back and slammed her forward into the cliff with him, hoping the kid didn't take them with him when he passed.

They felt the air rush past as he fell behind them to the bottom. His boot brushed the back of Kirk's uniform. The soft sound of contact made its way up to them. The kid was lying flat on his back. Eyes open. He'd fallen about a dozen meters to the ground.

Kirk scrambled down the rock. He dropped the last two meters and landed into a small depression, twisting his ankle. Kirk managed to stay on his feet, but pain shot up his leg. He'd worry about that after he checked on the kid.

"You okay?" Kirk reached for the kid's flare.

"Fine," he quickly replied, waving his hands at Kirk. "Fine! Don't call for help. Just had the wind knocked out of me."

"That was a long fall," Lynne said when she reached them.

"I'm fine," the kid insisted as he got up. He didn't even wince. "It's nothing. But we're losing time." He took off without another word.

Kirk shrugged at Lynne and followed after him, passing the kid with ease. He was moving slower, but he didn't seem to be in pain. Kirk, however, had banged up his ankle pretty badly, causing him to limp while he ran, but he wasn't about to let that stop him.

Now that they'd reached the bottom of the ravine, Kirk could finally see the finish line in the distance. A crowd of upperclassmen were gathered there, waiting to congratulate the winner. Kirk wanted to be the one accepting the adulation.

He tapped into his reserve energy and stepped up

his speed, pushing past the pain.

There were far fewer racers than there had been at the beginning. Only about a dozen cadets looked to have a shot at being the lone winner. Kirk caught up with Uhura, flashing her his winning smile. She rolled her eyes and kept up her pace, ignoring him.

Kirk was pretty sure he heard a laugh from Lynne.

The Andorian was still in the lead. He'd been at the front of the pack for almost the entire race, and didn't even seem winded. He was barely sweating. Kirk suspected that had something to do with his alien physiology. Andorians were known to perform pretty well in extreme conditions, like this desert heat.

With a final glance back at Lynne, Kirk dipped into the last of his reserve energy. Pumping his legs, he closed the distance between him and the Andorian. Kirk knew that he should pay more attention to the obstacles, but with the finish line in sight, he focused solely on getting there. He was ten long, painful, strides behind the Andorian. Whether or not Kirk fell into a hole or tripped over a rock didn't matter at this point. It was a flat-out race.

The Andorian clearly sensed Kirk's presence behind him. His muscular legs powered on, pulling him farther out in front.

Kirk doubled his effort, his own legs pumping harder still. Ankle throbbing. Panting breaths. Everything he'd ever learned about running went out of his head. It was just about getting to the end now.

The finish line was so close.

Kirk pushed himself as hard as he's ever had.

It wasn't enough.

The Andorian crossed the line three steps ahead of Kirk.

The upperclassman let out a cheer, and circled around the winner, congratulating him. Seconds later, Lynne and Kirk reached the finish line.

"Damn!" she shouted, kicking a rock and sending it flying. "We weren't even close."

One meter behind was pretty close as far as Kirk was concerned. "Hey, I don't like to lose, either, but second and third—"

"There's no second and third." She motioned to the Andorian and his admirers. "There's only first. The rest of us don't exist. Of course, if we had an Andorian's strengths, maybe we would have come in first, too. Probably used those antenna to sniff out obstacles on the course."

"Still, we did pretty well for humans," Kirk said lightly.

"Pretty well isn't good enough at the Academy," she said. Her tone was calm, but her words were full of anger. "We need to be at the top. That's going to be hard enough when we've got to compete with Andorian endurance or Vulcan logic. Or haven't you noticed how we're, like, the only humans in the group?"

Actually, Kirk hadn't noticed before, but he now saw that what she said was true. Uhura had come in with the next handful of racers along with the kid from the lunar colony. The four of them were among the few humans that had already made it to the finish. The rest of the racers were a collection of some of the tougher alien races in the universe.

"We've got four years to prove what we can do," Kirk reminded Lynne.

"I plan on being out of here in three," she said, echoing the same sentiment he had shared with Captain Pike when he'd joined up.

"That kind of commitment's not going to leave much time for a social life."

"You taking me out Friday night would go a long way in proving that wrong. And making me feel better."

Bold. He liked that. "Are you asking me on a date?"

"No," she replied. "I'm giving you permission to ask me out. There's a difference."

"Oh," Kirk said. "Good to know." He started to walk away. And felt the familiar tug at the back of his collar.

When he turned back to face Lynne, her eyes were glaring playfully.

"Now that you mention it," he said, "a night out would be the perfect way to end our first week here."

CH.3.28
Greeting Rituals

"Some other time, Thanas. I've got to get these greetings translated," Uhura said. Her fingers danced across the screen of her handheld Personal Access Display Device as she input the correct answers. Familiar alien greetings from the smooth, almost romantic Betazoid dialect to the hard consonants of the Denobulan language filled the screen.

Thanas tore the PADD from her hands and started typing on the touch screen. "Here, let me help. I know some very useful Andorian phrases."

"What are you, twelve? Give it back."

The smug grin on his face only annoyed her more. "Just a sec." The smile grew as he finished typing and handed the device back to her.

She knew she shouldn't read it, but it was impossible to delete the words without at least glancing at the screen. What he'd written wasn't as bad as Uhura had expected, but it wasn't anything she had any intention of agreeing to.

A swipe of her finger erased the suggestion from her assignment. The last thing she needed was her instructor seeing that.

"Very classy, Thanas." Annoying, too, since he'd erased her last answer in the process of trying to flirt with her. She retyped the Denobulan greeting, not sure if she was spelling it correctly. She'd have to come back to it later.

"Come on," he insisted. "Join me for lunch. Why is everyone so focused on studies here?"

Uhura turned her attention to the other students in the room. All the seats at every table in the vicinity were taken. Cadets were all hunched over their PADDs, the computer stations, and, in rare cases, books. Her table was the only one where a conversation was taking place. Unfortunately. "It *is* a library."

"Did you know on Risa the word 'library' means 'pleasure dome'?" Thanas said.

"You're making that up."

"Come to Risa with me and find out for yourself."

She had to give him credit for persistence. "Only if I need to find out the word for 'hello' there."

"Ah, that's the problem. They don't say it with words."

She almost laughed at that one. His attempts were irritating, but every now and then he hit on a good one. Under other circumstances she might have even given him a chance. But the first week at Starfleet Academy was not the time for starting a relationship. Not that she was under any impression that he was looking for a "relationship," considering all the other girls who had his attention.

Uhura turned *her* attention back to the assignment. It was pretty basic: translate the typical greeting of every member race in the United Federation of Planets into the equivalent greeting in English. She'd learned that in elementary school with the help of a universal translator. The challenge of this assignment came from being expected to do it from memory, without relying on technology.

However, that was not a very difficult task for Uhura. She'd even gone for extra credit by adding nonmember greetings, like Klingon, to the list. If she really wanted to show off, she'd throw in a little Romulan as well, but that one would actually take some research.

She suspected that the assignment was more of a test for the honor code than her memory. All these greetings could be easily found from a number of sources. Their instructor had specifically warned them that they were to complete the assignment from memory, not download the information from another source.

Thanas's pale blue hand slipped onto hers. It was not only uncomfortably forward of him, but it was stopping her from typing. "You've heard that old Earth expression about all work and no play, haven't you?" It was almost quaint how some aliens new to life on Earth had picked up on certain colloquialisms and used them as if they weren't tired old clichés. "Just a quick lunch."

Uhura had already grabbed that quick lunch consisting of a selection of alien cheeses and an apple that she could eat on her way to the library at the mess hall. She suspected that there would be many such lunches on the fly in her future. Only a few days in, and she was already buried in assignments.

Uhura slipped her hand out from under Thanas's. *Seriously. What's with these guys who don't take no for an answer?*

"Thanas, I have to finish this so I can start on those star charts for Astrosciences," she said firmly. "I'll see you in Interspecies Ethics."

That did the trick. Thanas left the table without another word. Actually, he kind of left in a bit of a huff. Probably not used to rejection. He'd been receiving a fair amount of attention since he won the survival course race at the start of the week. Why weren't those girls enough for him? Why did he have to keep going after her?

Uhura realized too late that they weren't in Interspecies Ethics together. It was Interspecies Protocol. Or maybe it was Combat Training. She hadn't wasted too much time memorizing the class rosters or even observing who was seated around her. Instead, she spent every class trying to keep up with the professor, from the moment she sat down to the moment she left the room.

Well, maybe Thanas was so insulted that he'd finally left her alone.

Doubtful.

The guilt over blowing him off eased some when Uhura saw him leave the library with two other female cadets. If he could attract women so easily, why was he so focused on her? Was it just about the chase with him? If she agreed to a date—*one* date—would he let it go?

Probably not. With Thanas, she doubted it was about dating. He was probably interested in more. And by *more*, she wasn't thinking "relationship."

It would be nice to be in a relationship. Not to feel so alone. Sure, she had already made friends at the Academy, but they were all so focused on their own agendas that they hadn't taken the time to know one another. It was only the first semester, but Uhura wondered if the feeling of being alone would ever go away.

"Thought he'd never leave," the guy sitting across from Uhura said. He was one of the younger cadets she'd seen at the Academy, not counting the fourteen-year-old wunderkind she'd met at orientation. This one was probably just out of high school.

She was embarrassed that her unwanted admirer had obviously been bothering her tablemate. "Sorry."

"Oh, no," he quickly said. "It's not your fault. You did everything you could to get rid of him short of stunning him with a phaser. Besides, I'm used to it. That great excuse for a cadet is my roommate."

"Really?" Thanas hadn't even said anything to the young cadet while he was at the table. It was kind of rude to totally ignore his roommate like that.

"I'm not sure he's noticed yet," he said. "After winning that stupid race, Thanas has been too busy fielding attention from everyone else at the Academy. He really only talks to me when he's kicking me out of the room so he and his latest girlfriend can be alone."

He'd pretty much just confirmed exactly what Uhura had suspected. If Thanas didn't have a chance before, he was certainly never going to get one now.

"By the way, if you want some extra credit on the language assignment, put in 'lunalai.'"

"Lunalai?"

"That's how we say hello on the moon," he said. "It's not technically another language, but maybe the instructor will get the joke." He pointed to the PADD where her assignment was clearly displayed on the screen. "But I'm not so sure Vulcans appreciate humor."

Uhura now knew why her tablemate looked familiar. He was in her Federation history class. He usually sat in the back, so it wasn't a surprise that she didn't recognize him right away. She held out her hand to him. "I'm Uhura."

"Jackson," he replied, reaching across the table.

As they shook, Uhura noticed a nasty bruise on his wrist, peeking out from the sleeve of his uniform. She immediately released his hand, worried that she was hurting him. "Oh, sorry," she said. "What happened?"

He seemed confused by the question at first, but realized she was looking at his wrist. "This? Nothing. Tripped. Still getting used to Earth's gravity."

"So, you're from the moon?"

"Grew up on the lunar colony. Artificial gravity doesn't pack the same punch as the real thing."

She couldn't take her eyes off the bruise. It was such a deep purple that it was almost black. "I'll say."

"It doesn't hurt," he said. "Honest."

"It looks broken," she said. "Couldn't they fix it at the infirmary?"

"Really," he insisted. "It's nothing."

He seemed increasingly uncomfortable with Uhura's concern. She didn't blame him. She didn't like it when other people focused on her weaknesses either. She wanted to change the subject, but she couldn't take her eyes off the bruise.

"You know, I'd better get going," he said, lifting his PADD with his bruised arm, as if to show her that he was fine. "I haven't eaten at all today. This place keeps me so busy, I keep forgetting."

"My stomach would never let me make that mistake," Uhura said.

He forced a smile, then made his way for the exit. Uhura silently cursed for allowing her curiosity to chase him away. Now she was scaring off potential friends. She could really use someone to talk to, who wasn't interested in hitting on her or showing off.

He really should have that bruise looked at, though.

She went back to the assignment, finishing up the last of the alien greetings when she felt a new presence hovering. Multiple presences, actually. When she looked up from her PADD, she saw four older cadets circling in that way people do when they want to seem casual even though they're really trying to intimidate you.

It wasn't that hard to figure out why. The math was simple enough: four cadets. Three empty chairs at her table.

Normally, she wouldn't give in so easily, but she'd finished the assignment, and was regretting choosing the library for studying.

She collected her belongings more slowly than she normally would, making them wait even longer for the table. *Serves them right for being rude.* Once she had the last of her things in her backpack, she rose from her chair and left.

The vultures descended before she was barely steps away. She shrugged them off as she made her way out of the library and into the brilliant sunshine of a San Francisco afternoon.

It seemed a waste to spend such a gorgeous lunch hour studying, but she had a week's worth of homework to plow through and only had a half hour of free time before her next class.

She would have gone back to her room, but spending time with Gaila, her roommate, was not conducive to studying. A nice enough girl, but her priorities were skewed. Partying was as important to her as passing. Uhura figured that there was a fifty-fifty chance she would graduate.

With her room out of the running, very few options were left. She could try to commandeer a classroom, but she'd probably spend the rest of the lunch hour trying to find an empty one. What she needed was someplace out of the way, where no one would bother her.

The observation deck!

The answer was so simple; she wasn't sure why she hadn't thought of it earlier. She'd been up to the observation deck on her orientation tour. The guide had told her group that it had the most spectacular view of Sausalito across the bay. She's also said that the only time anyone came up there was during the school tours, which happened in spring. The rest of the year, everyone was too busy studying to take the time to stop and enjoy the view.

It seemed unlikely that it was true, but Uhura decided to take a chance and check it out. The worst she would do is waste some time, and she was already doing that.

Uhura went back to the main building and took a turbo lift up to the topmost floor. She re-created the trip by memory since she hadn't been up there since her tour more than eight months earlier.

It was exactly where she remembered it and exactly *how* she'd been told it would be: totally empty.

She couldn't believe her luck. It was the quietest spot she'd found since she started at the Academy. Utterly silent and utterly empty. It didn't matter that there were no chairs. She slid down to the ground and set herself up in the corner, getting right to work on the rest of her assignments.

She didn't even look up once to glance at the view.

CH.4.28
Pain Management

Kirk ran his hands along Lynne's shoulders, kneading the muscles in her upper back. She looked very tempting dressed down in a white tank top and sweatpants. It was a nice change of pace from the standard red uniform he'd seen her in every other day of their first week at the Academy.

Even with his jacket unzipped, Kirk felt trapped in that very uniform. He was still dressed in the standard attire all the cadets wore on campus. Even though he wasn't usually one to care about fashion, it had already grown tiresome after one week.

There were variations on the uniform theme. The women wore skirts. The uniforms for physical activities were less restrictive. Blue uniforms were worn for command tests. It didn't make much difference. They'd all signed up for this monochromatic prison of conformity. At least it was comfortable.

His hands slipped down to the small of Lynne's back, running along the smooth fabric of her top.

He'd come over to her dorm room straight from his final class of the week. It was only meant to be a stop on his way to his quarters. A momentary distraction so they could firm up the details on their date later that evening.

Somehow, he hadn't managed to leave.

When Lynne had met him at the door, the exhaustion was clear on both their faces. As much as he wanted to spend time with her away from campus, he simply wasn't feeling the energy to get cleaned up and hit the town. A first date shouldn't feel like a chore, but the idea of doing anything that didn't involve sleep felt like too much work.

Lynne had felt the same way. Thankfully, she was the one to bring it up. The massage was Kirk's way of making up for not taking her out on that date.

Although, now that he was doing all the hard work, Kirk wasn't entirely sure that she was the one deserving the massage since she'd been the one to suggest they postpone the date. This was after she'd suggested the idea of a date in the first place. He didn't mind, though. He liked the feel of his hands on her skin, the warmth of her body heat radiating through the thin fabric of the shirt she wore.

His fingers explored the soft spots above her waist, tickling her gently as he went to wrap his arms around her neck in an embrace.

Lynne pulled away before he could entrap her, lying down on the bed in a closed-off manner. "Sorry," she said. "Not tonight, dear. I've got an entire body ache."

"Tell me about it," Kirk said dryly, rising off the bed to stretch out his right leg. His ankle had been bothering him on and off since the survival race the weekend before.

Lynne watched him as he paced the room. "You're limping again."

"Can't beat those advanced Starfleet observational skills," Kirk said with a wince. Every now and again the pain would shoot up his leg if he put it down wrong. "Think I aggravated it yesterday during drills in Basic Combat Training."

"You should get that checked," Lynne remarked.

"It's just a little pain," Kirk said. "Nothing to worry about." He'd been hurt worse before. Usually by other people. He wasn't about to show up in the infirmary because of a little ache. The last thing he needed was for word to get back to those guys who had attacked him back in Iowa. Kirk hadn't even seen them during the survival race, so they must have been way back in the pack. No surprise. They'd be the first ones wanting to see the son of George Kirk fail.

That wasn't going to happen.

"You know what they're doing, right?" Kirk said. "Trying to get us to pack it in the first week. See who washes out. They'll ease up after a while."

"Doubt that," Lynne said, sitting up. "The easing-up part. I'm with you on the idea that they're trying to force us to fail. But I don't have any intention of washing out. They can throw anything at me—a Klingon, even—I'll take them all on."

Kirk found her confidence attractive. He found a lot of things about her attractive.

"Why are you looking at me like that?" she asked.

"Why do you think?"

Lynne drifted back onto her bed. The move was more from exhaustion than enticement. "I don't know if I *can* think anymore. My brain is mush."

"I hear that," Kirk agreed. He'd been told before that his eyes were his best feature. He'd been aiming them at her with the full force of his seductive skills. He hadn't expected her to go jumping into his arms when he gave her his patented "Kirk stare," but he had hoped for a more welcoming response.

The Academy was already killing his mojo. How was he going to get through another three years of that?

He picked up the snow globe on her desk. Fittingly, it was a small model of Starfleet Academy, encased in glass and liquid. When he shook it, confetti rained around the campus. "Get this at the bookstore?"

When he received no response, he turned to see that Lynne's eyes were closed, her breathing shallow. She'd fallen asleep on him! Kirk sighed. This was shaping up to be the worst date ever, in spite of the fact that it wasn't technically a date.

Kirk tried not to take it personally. Her quiet snores were a result of the week they'd been through, not a reflection upon his company. Kirk considered curling up beside her. She looked so peaceful in her sleep. The softer side to the tough cadet he'd been getting to know. Like a concrete fist wrapped in a kidskin glove.

He stayed on his feet, not wanting to move too fast. They had only known each other a week. She might not appreciate him slipping into bed with her, even if his intentions were just to rest. He also didn't want to risk being found asleep when her roommate got back. The Academy had rules about cohabitating. Kirk didn't much care for those rules, but he didn't need to get into trouble his very first semester.

Kirk moved over to her window, debating if he should stay or go. She might only be out for a couple minutes. It wasn't worth calling it a night. Not yet, anyway.

Down on the quad, cadets dressed in uniform and in regular street clothes were making their way across the campus in the fading daylight. Some were on their way out for a night on the town. Upperclassmen mostly, Kirk figured. They were used to the intense training schedule by now. Plus, none of them were limping.

Millions of people across the universe would kill to gripe about their first semester at the Academy. For most people, getting into Starfleet wasn't as easy as just walking into a shuttle and saying, "Sign me up." Kirk had only managed to do that because the recruiting officer, Captain Pike, had vouched for him. The Kirk family name had carried him the rest of the way.

If he'd stopped to think about what he was signing up for, maybe he would have reconsidered. The first few months at Starfleet Academy had been more than he'd expected. The Desert Survival Course had only been the beginning.

Reveille was piped through the dorms PAs at 0530 every morning. It was a throwback to Earth traditions of old. Kirk wasn't exactly an early riser back home, but he managed to pull himself out of bed the Monday following the race, and immediately discovered that his banged-up ankle was going to be more of a problem than he'd thought. A quick sonic shower had relieved some of the pain, but not enough to get him moving at his usual pace.

Kirk hadn't been the only first-year cadet dragging that morning. Lynne had barely let out a groan when he passed her on the way to Exochemistry, although she had managed a smile that fueled him all the way to class.

The other first-year cadets in his seminar were just as groggy. He'd caught more than a couple of students dozing off, their chins dropping onto their chests.

Mornings didn't get any easier after that first one. The pain in his leg had mostly subsided—until that damned Andorian wrenched it again in Combat Training later in the week. The blue goon had been grandstanding to get some girl's attention.

Kirk couldn't *entirely* blame the guy. He'd been doing the same thing.

Lynne mumbled something in her sleep. Kirk couldn't make it out, but it pulled his thoughts back into the present. He really didn't want to spend his first free Friday night in San Francisco nursing his wounds in his dorm room. "Lynne," he said softly. "Monica?"

The only response was another indistinguishable mumble.

He'd wait her out a few more minutes. If she did wake up, maybe they could watch an old movie on the vid screen or something. That would make for a nice first date.

The lights came on across the Presidio, bathing the grounds in a white glow. He could make out part of the Golden Gate Bridge from Lynne's window. All he could see from his room was the wall of the administrators' building.

His thoughts drifted back to his first week at the Academy. His classes had been much harder than he'd thought they would be. He was already struggling to keep up.

Kirk would never admit that to anyone. In truth, there

was no one at the Academy he'd feel comfortable admitting it to. Kirk was never really big on friends back home. Most of the guys saw him as competition. For what, Kirk was never sure. He held his own with girls and at school, but he never really cared enough about anything to present a real challenge. It was more about the win with Kirk.

Could be that was why he had trouble making friends.

Griping about the Academy with Lynne was one thing. He wasn't ready to share with her the genuine fear he felt about not making it through. That was something he couldn't imagine sharing with anyone.

Sure, there was Leonard McCoy, or Bones, as he preferred to call his friend. Bones was as skeptical about the Academy rules and regulations as Kirk was, but he knew that Bones felt right about being there.

Kirk didn't always feel the same way. But where would he go if he didn't stay at Starfleet Academy? Back to Iowa? His stepfather had pretty much burned all of Kirk's bridges to home. With all the places on the planet he could live— all the places in the *universe*—he'd hung around the homestead far longer than he should have. Now that he was free, he could go anywhere.

He still couldn't believe he'd handed off his motorcycle to the first guy he saw before he boarded the Academy shuttle. Sometimes his "leap before you look" attitude led to regrets. Some regrets were immediate.

Some came later. But they always came.

He kissed Lynne on the forehead before making his way to the door. His date wasn't happening tonight. As he stepped into the hall, the pain in his ankle flared up again. He'd have to ice it when he got back to his room. Or was he supposed to put heat on it?

He didn't know.

Another couple weeks, Kirk thought. He'd give the Academy another couple weeks. Maybe a month, at the most. Then he could decide whether or not this place was right for him.

If it didn't kill him first.

CH.5.28
Observe and Report

Several weeks later . . .

The body lying on the biobed left an indistinct form in the sheet covering it. It wasn't clear if it was male or female, human or some other alien race. It just lay there, motionless.

McCoy couldn't believe it had already been a few weeks since he took that death trap of a shuttle to Starfleet Academy. And he still wasn't permitted to approach the body until after the senior medical officer entered the room.

It was worse than his days at medical school at the University of Mississippi. At least back then he'd been allowed to dissect a fetal pig in his first week.

McCoy hadn't realized when he signed up to be a medical officer just how much emphasis there'd be on the "officer" part. His days were filled with command training, combat lessons, and Federation rules and regulations. The bright spot came from the few advanced medical classes he had that had an emphasis on alien physiology.

He was learning more about alien races than he'd ever learned at his old school.

At Ole Miss, maybe eighty percent of his medical training had covered the human body. At the time, he'd had no plans to ever leave the planet Earth. The aviophobia he suffered from kept him on the ground, dreaming of living out his life as an old country doc.

He would have, too, if not for an ill-advised marriage at a young age, to a wife who eventually made him want to flee the planet. Divorce changed his plan of having a small-town medical practice and found him signing up for Starfleet Academy in the hope of finding a new dream.

As a member of Starfleet, McCoy was being exposed to many more alien races than he would in that small country town. The promise of travel to worlds that had yet to be discovered outweighed his fears of space travel. All those new peoples and new diseases. New weaponry that could be aimed at a starship. New biological warfare never even considered on Earth.

It was mind-boggling the number of ways a person could die in space.

What in the world was I thinking?

Death had brought McCoy back into an examination room today. His first autopsy as a Starfleet cadet. It was not on a fetal pig. That much he could tell from the outline of the body under the sheet.

Dr. Charles Griffin had been vague when assigning McCoy to this case. His instructor had waited until the last student filed out of Forensic Anthropology before he would even begin to explain why he'd held the cadet back. Even then, Griffin didn't say anything more than to order McCoy to go to exam room forty-seven and not tell anyone what he was up to.

That was the easiest part of the assignment. He didn't *know* what he was up to.

The door to the exam room opened, giving him a start. McCoy wasn't normally the nervous type. At least, not when he was firmly on the ground. But everything about this situation made him nervous. And suspicious.

"Marta?" McCoy wasn't expecting any other cadets, much less his surly lab partner.

"Dr. McCoy," she replied with a formal nod. Dr. Marta Peteque reminded McCoy more of a Vulcan than a human. In the short time that he'd known her, he'd never seen her crack a smile. Pity the poor patient who had to deal with her bedside manner.

"Need something?" he asked.

"I was looking for an open exam room to practice my diagnostics techniques." Her eyes gazed over McCoy's shoulder to the body on the table. "What's going on in here?" Peteque asked, her eyebrows raised.

"Just waiting for Dr. Griffin," he said.

She nodded to the body. "Extra credit?"

"Something like that," he said.

"Any reason you didn't think to include me?" she asked. "We *are* lab partners."

"Not my call," he said.

There were at a standstill. She clearly wanted to know more. McCoy didn't have anything else to tell her; wouldn't have said anything even if he did.

"Guess I'll try next door." She made a sharp turn, and left the exam room.

The door didn't even have time to shut before Dr. Griffin walked in. "What was Dr. Peteque doing in here?"

The abruptness of his question threw McCoy. "Said she was looking for a place to study."

"That didn't seem curious to you?" Griffin asked.

"No more than anything else going on here," McCoy replied. "Secret meetings in exam rooms. Unidentified bodies on the table. Feel like I've walked into some mystery."

"In a way you have," Griffin said as he moved over to the biobed. "Every autopsy is a mystery. The body has a wealth of clues to reveal to those who are paying attention."

Dr. Griffin conducted a mental inventory of the instruments on the table beside the biobed. It was the exact same thing McCoy did when he entered any exam room. When that was done, the doctor turned to face his student. "Sorry to be so secretive, but you'll understand why in a moment.

What I'm about to reveal must remain between us. I didn't want a student in on this autopsy, but the administration insisted. They see it as an important learning opportunity."

McCoy joined him at the exam table. "You've got my attention."

"Our findings today are going straight to the top at Starfleet Command," Griffin added, "so we must be precise."

Dr. Griffin placed the PADD he'd carried in with him on the table beside the body. He then carefully pulled down the top of the sheet, draping it at the waist. The deceased was a human male. Little older than a boy. McCoy understood at once why the autopsy was so important. "A cadet?"

Griffin nodded gravely. "First year."

McCoy had seen death before. He'd worked part-time at a retirement home when he was a teen. Back when he was still thinking about going into medicine. He'd gotten to know many of the residents. He became friends with them and lost more than a few of those friends. It was part of the reason he'd ultimately chosen the medical field.

This was different. This was a child lying naked and vulnerable on an exam table. McCoy knew that when he joined Starfleet, life wasn't going to be all sunshine and lollipops, but this was *school*. They were supposed to wash out before things got dangerous.

"Don't get ahead of yourself," Dr. Griffin warned.

McCoy often wore his emotions on his face. This time was no different. His anger was clearly evident. "What happened?"

"That's what we're here to determine," Dr. Griffin said as he prepped the body for autopsy scans, making sure there were no foreign objects present that could inhibit the scanners. "Cadet Jackson missed his first class this morning. When his roommate returned to their quarters, he was unable to wake the cadet. Emergency medical staff were called. They couldn't revive him. Must've died in his sleep."

"They couldn't determine the cause?" McCoy asked.

"Standard medical tricorders aren't always accurate on dead bodies," Griffin said. "You should know that."

Of course McCoy knew that. He was letting the shock of the deceased cadet get to him.

"The senior medical officer on duty stopped any further examination once mortem was determined," Dr. Griffin explained. "Standard operating procedure in any cadet death."

"*Any* cadet death?"

"It's rare," Dr. Griffin assured him, "but it does happen. And when it does, we take it seriously. Now, tell me your initial observations of the body."

McCoy's eyes met with Dr. Griffin's. His instructor betrayed no emotion about the situation. McCoy tried to mirror that in his own expression. How he behaved during this autopsy probably wouldn't be filed away in any official report, but Dr. Griffin would remember it.

McCoy moved toward the control module for the exam table. A series of monitoring devices were built into the wall to which the biobed was attached. He reached for the power switch to activate the unit.

Dr. Griffin held up a hand to stop him. "I'd like a visual inspection of the body first."

"Fine with me," McCoy said. He preferred to rely on his own skills to diagnose patients before trusting technology, anyway. Starfleet may have the most advanced medical equipment in the universe, but it seemed like nothing compared to good old horse sense.

"Go ahead," Griffin said. "Dazzle me."

McCoy stepped up to the body, conducting a visual inspection of the bare torso. "Patient is a human male, mid- to late teens—"

"You can skip the preliminaries," Griffin interrupted. "In the interest of expediency. The administration is waiting for our report."

McCoy moved on, citing the most noticeable piece of information. "Bruising along the obliquus externus. Looks mostly healed. Could have been in a fight, but it wasn't recent."

"No conclusions," Griffin warned. "Just observations."

"No other skin discoloration or visible abrasions on the

torso." McCoy moved to raise the arm.

"Don't touch the body, please. Just observe."

"Sir?"

"We should assume investigative protocols," Dr. Griffin explained. "If the cause of death does prove intentional, I do not want the administration questioning our procedures. I know you are an accomplished doctor, McCoy. But you are also a first-year cadet. We need to proceed carefully."

"Understood," McCoy said. It was a lie. The officers at the Academy sometimes treated McCoy as if he were no older than the boy on the slab. It was one of the downsides to his new career choice; starting over as if he was a fresh-man in med school.

"There appears to be some damage to the wrist," McCoy said. "Looks a few weeks old. Possibly broken and reset by an amateur, if it was reset at all."

Griffin nodded, moving in beside McCoy.

"A good start," Dr. Griffin said. "But we should get down to business. Please activate the medical scanners."

McCoy moved to the head of the table once again and turned on the power. The lights on-screen flashed in succession as the machine warmed up. The biobed was lined with scanners that would examine all points on the cadet's body, providing X-rays, ultrasound, chemical analysis, and a host of other exams. It allowed doctors to perform a complete autopsy without having to desecrate the remains by cutting into the deceased.

Medical science had advanced to the point where surgery could be performed, even broken bones set, without having to resort to the barbaric practice of slicing open the body. Some surgeons still liked to cut into their patients. McCoy never understood why. They likened it to an engineer pulling apart an engine to see how it worked. As far as he was concerned, that was not just unnecessary, but totally barbaric.

The diagnostic report came up on the monitor. Dr. Griffin was in front of McCoy before he had a chance to see the machine. "That can't be right." The senior officer started to punch commands onto the touch screen.

For a brief moment McCoy was offended by the implication he'd done something wrong. All he did was turn on the machine. But when the new readings came up, Griffin's reaction was the same. "That's impossible."

The doctor pushed past McCoy, laying his hands on the cadet's torso, making a tactile examination. "His insides are a mess," Griffin reported. "And don't think Starfleet will ever let you get away with a diagnosis like that yourself."

What McCoy saw on the monitor was unlike any diagnosis he'd seen in his limited years as a medical professional. Griffin was right. The cadet's internal organs *were* a mess; battered and bruised, swollen and torn. This couldn't have been the result of a single event. This damage was sustained over a period of weeks. Maybe more. Definitely since the start of the semester, if not before.

"There are wounds compounded on top of wounds," McCoy noted. "All of it went untreated. Why didn't anyone repair the damage?"

Griffin pounded his fist on the table. "Damned Starfleet."

McCoy understood the sentiment. He'd cursed Starfleet several times since he enlisted. He just didn't understand why Griffin was cursing them in this instance. "You're not suggesting that the med students ignored him, are you?"

"He wouldn't have been ignored if he didn't seek out treatment," Griffin said tersely as he completed his physical examination of the body. "You know how it is for cadets. No one wants to admit weakness. Why go to the doctor to ask for help? Especially if it's going to go on your record."

"He would have been in agony."

Griffin's eyes went wide. "Yes, he would have." He readjusted the scanners while mumbling words McCoy couldn't make out. A new set of readings came up on the screen. "And there's the answer."

McCoy did not understand what he was reading. "What is it?"

"The cadet had a congenital insensitivity to pain," Dr. Griffin said, pointing to the last line of the diagnosis.

McCoy searched his memory for the affliction. It seemed

familiar, but he couldn't place it. "I don't know that one."

"Why would you?" Griffin asked. "It was cured more than a century ago. The Vulcans actually gave us the information that led us to permanently eradicate it. Even before that, it was incredibly rare. I doubt one doctor in a hundred had even heard of it."

Just because this affliction hadn't been seen on Earth in a century was no excuse for McCoy to be unfamiliar with it. He promised himself that he would look up everything about it once they were done. No chance he was going to be caught unprepared again.

"A person who is born with the affliction suffers from a severe loss of sensory perception. The nerve fibers of the body malfunction. The cadet was physically incapable of feeling pain."

McCoy easily made the connection. "So if he was injured in training, he wouldn't have thought anything was wrong. Wouldn't have known that he had to get treatment."

"He would have thought he was invincible," Griffin said. "Like all the other cadets."

"But how would something like this go untreated for so long?" McCoy asked. "How did they miss it in the Starfleet physical?"

Dr. Griffin fell into an uncomfortable silence. Most likely deciding whether or not to continue the examination with a cadet in the room. If the conclusion reflected poorly on Starfleet, it would probably be best for Griffin to keep it to himself.

He let out a sigh. "They missed it because they wanted to. Half the doctors that perform the physical only see what they want to. Have to get those recruiting numbers up. The other half sees everything that could possibly be wrong with you. Make note of the tiniest flaw."

McCoy must have gotten one of the more serious physicians. His exam upon acceptance was one of the most thoroughly invasive procedures he'd ever undergone. They checked back to his great-grandfather's records for any genetic conditions. As far as he knew from what he'd heard from the other cadets, they'd experienced the same thing. He guessed it made sense that medical officers would be more thorough with medical cadets. The lazier doctors probably got the cadets who didn't notice they were cutting corners.

McCoy moved closer to the monitor, wanting to take in every salient detail. Even though the odds were against him ever coming across this affliction again, it wouldn't hurt to commit the signs to memory. It was only through his thorough examination of the scans that he caught something he hadn't noticed the first time.

"Sir," McCoy said, "I think you should see this."

"What now?"

McCoy didn't want to say what he was thinking. It was

too horrible to suggest out loud. "Unless I'm mistaken, I don't think this was a natural occurrence."

"What are you talking about?"

McCoy raised a finger to one of the scans of the body, enlarging it to a magnitude of ten. "See here? There's evidence of microsurgery on the nerve fibers. Which means it was done intentionally. Within the past few months. Maybe the past few weeks."

The blood drained from Dr. Griffin's face. He looked physically ill. McCoy couldn't blame him for the reaction. The implications were sickening.

"Someone did this to him. Someone operated on his nerve fibers," McCoy repeated. "But why?"

Dr. Griffin grabbed a chair to steady himself. He took a deep breath before he said, "If he didn't feel the pain, he didn't stand out from his peers. Didn't risk washing out."

"But just because he didn't feel the pain, doesn't mean that his body wasn't hurting," McCoy said. This revelation caused Griffin to collapse into the chair as McCoy paced the room, unable to contain his anger. "Whoever performed this surgery would have been an idiot!"

"That he would. He'd also be a criminal," Dr. Griffin said with a nod.

CH.6.28
Interspecies Protocol

Uhura let out a frustrated yell. She could do that since she was by herself. *Blissfully alone*. Finding the observation deck was the best thing she'd done in her first months at Starfleet Academy. It was the one spot where she didn't have to contend with a partying roommate or an Andorian who wouldn't leave her alone.

Unfortunately, the solitude wasn't helping her find the right answers for her assignment for Interspecies Protocol.

Alien languages had never been a problem for her. She'd always had a natural inclination toward the different ways the races of the Federation communicated. As a child, her parents used to bring her out at dinner parties to impress their friends with her knowledge of different alien languages. She could silence a room with an obscure Tellarite dialect, but learning proper protocol for interacting with alien races was proving to be a surprising challenge.

It was weird. She was usually so good at reading people

when they were in front of her. The seemingly endless minutiae of alien customs and practices she had to memorize was mind-boggling.

Uhura had always been confident that she'd never offended anyone with her words. Her actions were another matter entirely. There were so many ways a Starfleet officer could start an intergalactic incident just by reaching out to shake an alien hand.

Something I should never do on the planet Glakota. Or was it Narudian IV?

She scanned down the page on her PADD and confirmed that it was Narudian IV where an outstretched hand was perceived as an act of war. On Glakota it was an invitation to a private rendezvous.

Also something I might want to avoid.

She placed the PADD on the ground. It was time for a break. Pulling up her legs in front of her, she rested her elbows on her knees and dropped her head into her hands. She could've spent the rest of the afternoon curled up in a ball on the floor of the observation deck. No one would notice. No one would miss her, either. Her classmates were all so wrapped up in their own lives that it could take days to report her disappearance.

That would be nice. To disappear for days.

It would be so much easier to learn these things through practical methods, to interact with the alien races in question. Sure, she had many classmates from different worlds in the Federation, but most of them were impossible to study with. She might get through one full page of reading before they wanted to gossip about the latest rumors overheard on campus.

Or there were the others. The cadets who considered the Academy a battleground. Their peers were enemies, fighting to graduate at the top of the class. They refused to study together, not wanting to give their competition any advantage over them.

That was why it was easier to study in the privacy of the observation desk. Easier, but not more helpful.

She closed her eyes to rest for a moment. She'd stayed up late studying for a Xenolinguistics exam, and didn't want to tax her mind too much. She could already feel the stress settling in. Starfleet Academy was exactly as difficult as she'd expected it to be, which was a shame. She'd really hoped that she'd been psyching herself up with images of the worst-case scenario.

Uhura hadn't meant to doze off, but she woke with a start when the door to the observation deck opened. She looked up to see a tall Vulcan male in a dark uniform standing over her.

She jumped to her feet before the sleep had even cleared from her eyes. "Commander Spock!"

"Cadet Uhura," Spock said, greeting her with a nod.

"I apologize for disturbing you . . ."

"No," she said quickly. "Not disturbing at all. I was just studying. Studying for your class." She was usually much better with her words than that. Especially when speaking in her native language. She was just awfully embarrassed that an instructor had caught her napping in public, such as it were.

They both looked down at the PADD on the ground. It was in sleep mode. The screen was blank. Great. Just what she needed. One of her instructors thinking she was goofing off.

There's always a chance he thought she was going over her studies in her head.

"I understand," he said. "When I was a cadet, I found the lack of distractions in the observation deck to be beneficial in my studies. I often came here seeking solitude."

"Exactly," she said, glad that he understood why she was randomly there on the floor.

"And on several occasions fell asleep here as well," he added.

She should have known there was no fooling a Vulcan. "It was just for a few minutes," she said.

"Perfectly understandable," Spock said. "Cadets often find the first year at the Academy to be an exhausting experience. The curriculum is designed that way to weed out the less committed students."

She'd suspected as much, but it was still odd to hear a member of the faculty admit it. Then again, he'd just graduated, so it made sense that he'd understand what she was feeling.

Odd that she'd think that about a Vulcan. Their race was known for the suppression of emotions. She'd heard that he was half-human, but she'd never seen that side of him in class. Yet he'd cut right to the heart of her issue.

She wondered what else was going on beneath that surface. Had he come to the observation deck for solitude, like he had when he was a cadet. Or was he there to enjoy the view. The latter seemed unlikely.

"I guess I should get going," she said. She had a free period after lunch, so she didn't need to leave, but she felt like she was intruding on his time—even though she was the one who'd gotten there first.

"That is not necessary," Spock said. "I clearly have interrupted . . . your studies."

"The impromptu nap interrupted that," she said. "But I should get back to your assignment."

"Yes," he said. "I have heard that I am quite the taskmaster."

Was he making a joke? A Vulcan who understood humor? Maybe there was more to that human side of him.

"It seems we have both come here for the same reason," Spock said. "To work in solitude. If that is the case, I do not see why we cannot work in solitude together."

"I thought all the instructors had their own offices."

"Work is being done on mine at the moment," he said. "The environmental controls are malfunctioning. The temperature is currently set to below freezing."

She could see how that would be especially problematic for someone from a desert climate. That explained why their paths hadn't crossed in the observation deck in the past three weeks. "Well, pull up some floor," she said as she went back down to get her PADD.

"Actually, I have found the ledge by the window to be more suitable to my needs," he said as he moved over to the glass picture window. A metal ledge ran along the window at waist level. It looked like anyone who sat on it would have to perform quite the balancing act.

The skepticism must have shown on her face, because Spock explained as he sat. "It is best to sit in the corner," he said. "Lean back, and use the wall to prop yourself up. It is actually quite comfortable. Certainly more comfortable than the floor."

He did look comfortable in the little cubby that formed where the wall, window, and ledge met. She got up and mimicked his position on the opposite end of the window, leaning her back against the glass. He was right. It was a better choice than the floor. "Thanks."

They sat at the window, across from each other.

Their backs were to the view and their heads down on their work, focused on their respective projects in quiet contemplation. They sat working for the better part of an hour, until they were interrupted by the tweet of the communicator attached to Spock's belt. In the silence of the observation deck, it sounded as loud as the red alert Klaxon on a starship.

Spock wore an almost sheepish expression as he grabbed the device and opened it. "Spock here."

"Commander Spock," a voice said from the communicator. "Please report to Admiral Bennett's office."

"Acknowledged," he replied, signing off without another word.

Uhura looked up from her PADD. She'd seen the Academy dean speak several times in front of the students, but she'd never met him in person. She assumed the faculty interacted with him more often, but it was still impressive that Spock was being called to meet with the admiral.

The abruptness of the conversation was equally as interesting. If someone had ordered her to the admiral's office, she surely would have had a few questions for whomever was on the other end of the line.

There did seem to be a glimmer of puzzlement on Spock's face as he rose from the ledge. It probably wasn't every day that he had an audience with the admiral, Uhura thought as she grew more curious about the call.

"Thank you for sharing your study space with me," Spock said.

"It was yours first," she said. "Guess I was just keeping an eye on it for you."

"I am certain that it is now in capable hands," Spock replied.

She tried to contain herself as he left. A compliment from a Vulcan! She wasn't even sure that they were able to do such a thing.

It was interesting. There had been nothing particularly special about their encounter. And yet, after spending a little time in Spock's company, Uhura found herself feeling like she had a better grasp of Interspecies Protocol.

CH.7.28
The Academy Mess

Kirk slipped an extra chocolate chip cookie into the pocket of his uniform and continued down the mess hall line. It wasn't stealing since the cadets' meals were provided for them, but he had to hide it nonetheless. The Academy kept strict control over the students' calorie intake. An extra dessert would be recorded in his file.

Yet another reason he thought Starfleet might not be the right place for him. Even his dessert came with rules.

He still hadn't decided exactly how he felt about the Academy. For every success he'd had over the past months, there'd been an equal failure. In some classes he shined. In others, he was struggling. The only bright side was that his ankle had healed on its own.

Kirk slid his tray through the scanner, placed his thumb on the monitor, and recorded his calorie intake. He grabbed another cookie on the way back to the table. It wasn't that Kirk had much of a sweet tooth. He just didn't like being told what to do.

"Dessert?" Lynne asked when he reached their table. A pile of brownies sat in the empty spot across from her. He wasn't the only one who appreciated minor rebellions.

He added his cookies to the pile. "It's like we're both eight, and our mothers told us to keep our hands out of the cookie jar."

"Don't know any eight-year-old who could get a perfect score on the phaser firing range on her first try."

"Still bragging about that?"

"And I plan to keep bragging about it until you beat my record time," Lynne retorted. "Or until you take me out on that date you've been promising me."

Kirk motioned to the packed mess hall. Dozens of conversations echoed around the room as the cadets sat under the harsh institutional lighting. "What? We've got food. We've got ambiance. You don't consider this a date?"

"No."

"What about the night we went stargazing with the astronomy class?"

"No."

He leaned across the table. "Or how 'bout that time we—"

She pushed him back. "Definitely not."

"Then I give up," he said, digging into his lunch. "I'm turning over the date planning to you."

"That's not very gentlemanly."

"And here I thought you were a modern woman," Kirk said. "Besides, you're the one who brought up this whole dating thing in the first place."

"Is that your way of telling me you're not interested?"

"It's my way of telling you that maybe *I'd* liked to be wooed a little. I'd like to be the one getting the massage."

Lynne raised an arm and waved across the mess hall. "Thanas!"

Kirk's fork landed on his tray with a *clank*. "Is this your way of telling me you've moved on?"

"With Thanas?" she asked. "Have you lost your mind?"

"You called him over here," Kirk reminded her. "Him and his legion of followers."

The Andorian's popularity had dipped in recent days. It had been more than two months since he won the survival course. He hadn't really done anything to make himself stand out since then. Everyone else was pretty much focusing on their own accomplishments. At least Kirk was. Still, he was annoyed to see that the guy had a few hangers-on still following him to their table.

"You know what they say about keeping your friends close and your enemies closer?" Lynne replied right before Thanas arrived.

"Monica," the Andorian said with a leer.

Kirk didn't like how Thanas was calling Lynne by her

first name. It was a tradition to refer to one another by surnames in Starfleet, especially while in uniform. It was a sign of respect. Certainly, Kirk called her Monica on occasion, but that was during more personal moments. Not when he was greeting her in a packed mess hall.

If he were being honest, Kirk would have acknowledged to himself that he didn't care about tradition. He was jealous. There was no reason to be, but jealousy rarely followed reason.

"Thanas," she replied curtly. "You know Jim Kirk?"

They exchanged nods of greeting. They knew each other all too well. Their paths had crossed several times in Combat Training. Usually with painful results.

Thanas sat beside Lynne. He'd brought three friends with him. There were only two open seats. Kirk watched with annoyance as Thanas's female followers jockeyed for a position through a game of musical mess hall chairs, except without the music. A cute, red-headed, green-skinned Orion girl was the one left standing. Kirk could tell she was vacillating between finding a chair and forcing her way into the group, or leaving.

She made up her mind, moving on without a word. Kirk was glad to see that she recovered quickly, finding a guy at the next table who was willing to open up a space for her when she flashed him a flirty smile. Thanas didn't even notice she had gone.

"You guys hear the news?" Thanas asked.

"What news?" Lynne responded.

"'Bout my roommate," he said. "Jackson."

Kirk and Lynne shared a look. They hadn't heard anything, but neither of them wanted to prod Thanas on. He was obviously parsing out the information in a way that would keep him the center of attention for the longest time possible.

Thankfully, one of his admirers filled that role. "What about him?" Karin Andros asked between bites. Her tray was overloaded with food, and she was eating like it was the only meal she was going to take time out of her day for. Out of her week, really, considering how quickly she was scarfing down the food. Eating that way could *not* be healthy.

"Died," Thanas said. "This morning. Or last night. Not quite sure."

Everyone at the table froze, except Thanas. He'd actually taken that moment to start eating. Kirk wanted to smack him for being so blasé. "A cadet died? How? What happened?"

Thanas shrugged between bites. "Beats me. Probably allergic to gravity. He was from your lunar colony."

Kirk wondered if he was the same kid who fell during the survival course. The lunar colony wasn't that populated. Couldn't be that many cadets from there. The odds were good that it was the same person.

The fall had been pretty bad, but he'd seen the cadet around campus since then. He didn't seem to be in any pain. "Why haven't we heard anything about it? None of my instructors have said anything."

"Mine either," Lynne agreed.

"You think admin wants this thing to get around?" Thanas scoffed. "Only reason I know is because I found him. Being he was my roommate and all. Wonder if this means I get all As for the semester." He looked to the girls flanking him. "Isn't that the rule if your roommate dies?"

Nobody could answer his question. Probably since everyone was so horrified that he could turn news of his roommate's death into something about him.

Lynne dropped her fork onto her tray. "Think I just lost my appetite."

"Really?" Thanas said, missing the point. "Didn't peg you for the sensitive type." He nodded. "I like that."

"Excuse me," Lynne said as she grabbed her tray, and got up.

Kirk still had his appetite, but wasn't about to spend the rest of lunch with Thanas and his fan club. He took one last heaping bite of his pasta, wrapped a brownie in a napkin, and followed Lynne with his tray.

She was dropping her food into a composting station when he reached her. "He's a pig."

"No argument from me," Kirk said. He didn't think reminding her that she was the one who had called Thanas over in the first place was a good idea. "You think he was on the level about Jackson?"

Lynne grabbed a pear on her way out to the quad. "Don't know why he'd lie about it. Then again, I don't get much of what Thanas does."

The campus grounds were buzzing with students and faculty going about their day in the beautiful San Francisco sunshine. People were laughing, rushing to class. A pickup game of flag football had broken out.

Not a single sign that death had visited the campus last night.

Kirk wondered if the administration could really cover up something like that. It didn't seem likely. Word was bound to spread, especially with someone like Thanas in on the news.

Lynne and Kirk walked in silence while they both thought over what they'd been told. It was another strike against the Academy in Kirk's eyes. He'd expected the place to be tough, but never imagined it would kill anyone. Of course, he didn't know that the kid died because of the Academy. It could have been a totally unrelated event.

Somehow he doubted that.

"Let's focus on a happier note," Lynne said. "Our date?"

"Uh-uh," Kirk said. "I've decided I want you to surprise

me. Please show me how easy it is to put something together, considering our busy schedules."

"I accept your challenge," she said with a bow. "Block out your evening. I've already got an idea."

"Today?" Kirk had two different study groups this afternoon. Since he couldn't remember what classes either was for, he figured that he could probably blow them off. If that meant getting to spend some time alone with Lynne, he would definitely do it. His smile gave her his answer.

"Okay, then," she said as she started off. "I'll send you the details later."

He called after her. "Remember, I expect to be impressed."

She threw him a backward wave as she took off toward the student union. Kirk watched her leave. Though he still felt badly for the kid that he hardly knew, Kirk also felt like he had something to look forward to in this place. That alone brightened his mood dramatically.

CH.8.28
Official Investigation

"Commander Spock, I'm sure you're wondering why you've been called to the principal's office." Admiral Richard Bennett said from behind his desk. He sat between that desk and a large picture window that overlooked half the campus. The office was by far the largest and most extravagantly decorated in the administration building.

Spock assumed the "principal's office" reference was a quaint colloquialism, the kind he often heard while on Earth.

In the few years Spock had spent living on his mother's home world, he'd come to accept the fact that humans overly relied on culturally specific references, expecting those who did not grow up on their world to understand them. In his early days as an Academy cadet, Spock had to endure the somewhat condescending glares from his peers when he interpreted a comment too literally or simply misunderstood a reference. He endeavored not to make that mistake in front of the dean of Starfleet Academy.

Instead, he focused on the point of Bennett's question. "I find conjecturing on such matter to be a distraction. I see no reason to wonder about an issue that you will surely reveal to me at the proper time."

"Well, be that as it may, I'm sure you understand how well regarded you are by the rest of the faculty here."

"Yes," Spock replied.

The dean paused. Spock's response seemed to catch him off guard. It was possible that the admiral had anticipated an expression of gratitude for his compliment.

On Vulcan, Spock's instructors had never expected to hear a "thank you" for a mere assessment of his superior work. The admiral was just relaying information that had been passed along by his subordinates. Still, the silence that was building was growing noticeable.

Spock pushed aside the logical response in favor of meeting the requirements of Earth customs. "Thank you."

This elicited a smile from the admiral and allowed him to proceed. "Impressive, indeed. First Vulcan cadet at Starfleet. Graduated at the top of the class. And, of course, programming the Kobayashi Maru scenario in your senior year. That was a feat of considerable achievement."

Another pause.

"Thank you."

"And now the head of your department tells me that you have proposed some truly advanced plans for your classes. A great start to the school year."

A third pause.

This was growing tiresome.

"Thank you."

"Which leads me to my unorthodox request," Bennett said, pausing for a second. "A situation arose this morning. Something that may be a unique incident . . . or possibly the sign of a deeper problem."

Spock noticed that the admiral was choosing his words carefully. Being intentionally vague as if he did not wish to address this mysterious "situation." It was odd, considering it was the very subject Spock had been called into the office to discuss.

A soft whooshing sound alerted him that the door behind him had opened. He rose along with the dean. "Captain Warde, thank you for joining us," Admiral Bennett said. "You know Commander Spock?"

"Certainly," she said as the pair exchanged greetings. Warde had been one of Spock's instructors during his first year at Starfleet Academy, back when she was still a lieutenant commander. She'd been the Academy's leading expert on Federation law and security training.

If Spock had such a thing as a "favorite" teacher, she would have qualified. When she was known as Lieutenant

Commander Warde, she was one of the few instructors who hadn't been intimidated by his intellect upon their first meeting. What other members of the faculty had mistaken for arrogance on his part, she insightfully understood was merely his way of clearly delineating his thought process without needless emotion.

Warde had left Starfleet Academy after Spock's first year as a cadet to serve as Chief of Security on the USS *Exeter*. It was curious that she would return before her five-year mission on the starship was complete. Her promotion to captain suggested that her shorter service had been exemplary.

"Please have a seat," the admiral said, resuming his position behind his desk. "Captain Warde, perhaps you could bring Spock here up to speed on the case you are investigating."

The captain dove right in to her story without preamble, providing Spock with the details of the death of one Cadet Jackson. She listed the collection of wounds that were discovered during the autopsy, along with the evidence of questionable surgical practices. Warde ran through the facts without comment or unnecessary emotion, laying out the situation in a concise manner that Spock found refreshing. She ended with a simple question. "Your thoughts?"

Spock considered the facts. "It is not surprising that a

weaker student might try to find a way to enhance his abilities," he said. "Starfleet Academy is one of the foremost
institutions in the galaxy."

"Thank you," the admiral said, throwing Spock off
momentarily by the unexpected interruption.

"However, it must be noted that the cadet's chosen course of action was particularly ill-advised," Spock
continued.

"Don't be so polite, Spock," Captain Warde interjected,
throwing her first real emotion into the proceedings. "It
was stupid. Pure and simple."

The admiral cleared his throat.

"But while Cadet Jackson's behavior was fatally *ill-
advised*," she continued, "I'm more bothered by the fact
that whoever performed this surgery had to know what
he or she was doing. This is an advanced procedure. The
doctor—and I'm using that term loosely—had to be aware
that stopping Jackson from feeling pain was not helping
him in any way. Yet the doctor performed the operation
anyway. To what purpose?"

Spock considered that line of thought. "You fear
that the culprit might attempt the same surgery with
another cadet?"

"We do," Captain Warde said. "And it just doesn't feel
right in my gut. It's a very random procedure. I think there
might be more to this."

Spock ignored most humans when they referred to their "gut" in any decision-making endeavor. Captain Warde, however, was different. She didn't jump to a conclusion without fully examining the situation. Where other people often followed their gut to the exclusion of actual facts, she only used it as a starting point.

The admiral cautioned, "No need to get ahead of ourselves. This is just the start of the investigation. But you can see, Spock, how we would want to get in front of this before word spreads to the students."

"You intend to keep the cadet's death a secret?" Spock asked. While that might help the investigation, Spock could not imagine that it was a wise course of action. In his time at the Academy, he had learned that most news the administration tried to keep classified often spread even faster.

"Not at all," Admiral Bennett said.

"We're waiting until the cadet's parents can be notified," Warde explained. "They're on holiday off planet, and we haven't been able to contact them."

The admiral straightened in his seat. "We'd like you to assist the captain in her investigation, Spock. I feel that a Vulcan perspective will be invaluable. It's also nice to have someone a bit closer to the cadets' ages involved. Maybe get some insight into their thinking. See if you can use that to your advantage."

Spock wasn't entirely sure what the dean was suggesting, but he nodded in agreement.

"I'll leave you two to discuss how to proceed." Admiral Bennett dismissed them with a nod toward the door.

Spock accompanied Warde in total silence as they walked through the outer office, passed the dean's assistant, and went out into the crowded halls. That silence stayed with them all the way to Captain Warde's office since she would not discuss the case in front of others. Spock appreciated that Warde did not bother to engage in small talk in the meantime.

Her office was not as decorated as the admiral's nor was it as large. Spock was not sure if Captain Warde's design aesthetic tended toward the spartan or if she simply had not yet unpacked her personal items. He'd had no reason to visit her office when he was a cadet.

As soon as the door was shut behind them, Captain Warde addressed their working situation. "I'm going to be honest with you, Spock."

He had learned to be suspicious of that phrase during his time on Earth. Spock found that when a human felt the need to point out that they were being honest, it usually meant they were about to be insulting.

The captain took a seat behind her desk. "I didn't want you on this investigation," she said. "I *don't* want you on the case."

Spock raised a questioning eyebrow, but remained silent while she explained.

"Not that I don't think you will provide valuable assistance," she added. "A Vulcan perspective will be an asset. But I was hoping for someone who could blend in with the cadets. Speak to them on their level. Interact as a peer. I don't think I'm saying anything surprising when I point out that you don't exactly blend in."

"My time at the Academy has more than adequately prepared me for that criticism."

"It's not criticism, Spock," she insisted. "It's just a statement of fact. I'm sure you will prove to be exceedingly useful to the investigation. I just haven't figured out how yet."

Spock would have suggested any number of contributions he could make to the case, but he suspected it would have been irrelevant. Captain Warde was well acquainted with his abilities from his years as a cadet, and likely had studied up on his more recent accomplishments before meeting in the admiral's office.

"I have a couple quick interviews I need to conduct," Warde said, handing him a PADD. "Here are the initial notes on the investigation, along with the cadet's files and other pertinent information. It's all been pulled together in the past hour so don't expect much." She got up and went for her door. "I'll be back shortly."

Spock nodded, then got to work reading through the

files. She was right in saying that the information was limited. After all, it was only the beginning of the investigation.

He did understand what she'd been saying about his inability to blend in. Like the "gut feeling" that the captain had referenced earlier, this was a quality that had escaped him during his time as a cadet. Building relationships with the more highly emotional races of the Federation had often proven to be the more challenging aspect of his time there.

Spock appreciated a challenge, though. This would simply be another in a long line of obstacles he had overcome since moving to Earth. He was looking forward to the opportunity to prove himself in any situation that would test his abilities. He was particularly intrigued by this investigation, because it seemed like a chance for him to tap into his human side. Not something he often attempted.

CH.9.28
Questions and Answers

McCoy knew the moment he connected the dots on the illegal surgery performed on the deceased cadet that he'd stepped into a mess of trouble. First-year cadets shouldn't get involved in scandals. Even by accident. It wasn't good for career advancement.

Things moved very quickly in the moments after Griffin reported their findings to his superiors. Admiral Bennett had been the first on the scene, demanding to be walked through the autopsy. Several other senior officers stormed into the room in the minutes that followed, requesting the same information.

This was before they'd even noticed McCoy. The questioning stopped immediately, and McCoy was instructed to wait in Dr. Griffin's office. He was told not to leave for any reason.

That was more than two hours ago.

McCoy was still waiting.

His thoughts turned, once again, to that small medical practice somewhere in the country he'd always dreamed of opening. A place where he would treat patients from birth to adulthood. Where the diagnoses would fall into categories of illness people had been suffering with for generations, not mysterious criminal causes. Where he wouldn't have to deal with the bureaucracy of big city hospitals.

Those hospitals were now a dream compared to the levels of political red tape he suspected he was about to experience with Starfleet Academy.

Dr. Griffin finally returned to his office, carrying a mug of coffee. McCoy was up and out of the guest chair the moment the door opened.

"Sorry you were stuck waiting," Dr. Griffin said as he took a seat on the couch. "Seems we've stirred up quite a bit of a hornet's nest."

"I'd guess so," McCoy said. He joined his mentor on the couch. "At least the administration is taking this seriously."

"Oh, they're taking it very seriously," Griffin reassured. "These kinds of things don't usually happen in a vacuum."

McCoy assumed the administration would want to keep this investigation contained to the Academy, but he wasn't so sure it could be. Cadet Jackson's death wasn't just an unfortunate training accident. It was possibly a symptom of a problem that ran much deeper. "You think something bigger's going on?" McCoy asked. "What's the administration going to do about it?"

"Captain Warde's been assigned to head up the investigation," Griffin said. "As to what she's doing, you'll find out soon enough. She wants to see you in the faculty conference room in the administration building in five minutes."

"Me?"

"You were the one who diagnosed the problem," Griffin reminded him. "Kind of your fault we're all involved, isn't it?"

McCoy knew that Griffin was making a joke, but he didn't find it all that funny. "When I'm done, you want me to come back here and fill you in?"

"No. I've got an errand to run," Griffin replied, "Report to emergency medical services. You did a good job this morning. I'm putting you on emergency room rotation."

"Thank you, sir." McCoy couldn't believe it. As horrible as his findings were this morning, he never expected to be rewarded simply for catching something his instructor had not.

"You better get moving," Griffin suggested. "Admin isn't exactly next door."

McCoy wanted to ask the doctor more about what the investigators were thinking. He wanted some idea of what he was walking into. It wasn't that McCoy was concerned about saying or doing the wrong thing. He knew he'd already been helpful. Being effectively held captive in

Griffin's office for two hours made him uncomfortable. No telling how long the investigating officer might keep him.

That was especially troubling now that he had something to look forward to once the interview was over. Not for the first time, McCoy realized that doctors had an odd perspective on life.

McCoy left the Starfleet medical building and made his way across campus. He wondered if any of the other cadets he'd passed knew about what was happening around them. The odds were good that word had spread by now. Even in a structured organization like Starfleet, gossip could not be contained. This kind of story was exactly the type that set the grapevine abuzz.

McCoy's wandering mind stopped short outside the conference room when he saw Dr. Peteque stepping into the hall. He couldn't imagine what she was doing there.

The way she exploded in semicontained rage upon seeing him gave him his answer. "Why would you tell Griffin that I was snooping around your little whatever it is you were doing earlier?"

"I just told him you'd been there. Didn't say you were up to anything." McCoy was pretty sure that Griffin had seen her leave the room himself. All McCoy had done was pass along what she'd told him.

"And yet suddenly I'm getting called to the administration building to answer a bunch of questions," she said, "just for walking into a room I thought was empty. What's going on?"

If Captain Warde hadn't seen fit to explain the situation to Peteque, McCoy wasn't about to. "Got me," he said as he brushed past her. "Now if you'll excuse me, I hear the good captain has some questions for me as well."

McCoy knew that his blithe manner would only annoy Peteque even more. And it did. She stormed off in a huff that was very unlike the behavior of most grown medical students.

Once Peteque was gone, McCoy stepped up to the conference room door, bracing himself for whatever was on the other side. He expected a packed house. This kind of thing would have the administration doubling and tripling up to make sure that the investigation was well covered. He took a deep breath as the sensor on the door registered his presence.

This is not going to be fun.

The first surprise came as soon as the door swished open, revealing a nearly empty conference room. A woman McCoy assumed to be Captain Warde sat at the near end of a long conference table. He'd never met the captain in person, but he'd seen her name on the class schedule. She taught law classes and security officer training. She was the natural choice to lead this kind of investigation.

"Cadet McCoy." Warde remained in her chair, but her greeting was warm. "Have a seat." She motioned to the

chair beside her. He'd half expected her to be on one side of the table while he sat on the other side. That seemed more proper to an investigation. This seating arrangement was more casual, which put him on higher alert than he would have been in a formal setting.

"Captain Warde," McCoy said as he sat.

"I've heard some good things about you, McCoy," she began. "Sorry we're not meeting under more fortunate circumstances."

"Well, I figure my medical studies keep me busy enough," McCoy replied. "Not much chance I can take on law classes to add to the workload."

Captain Warde got right to the point. "Can you please walk me through your autopsy on the body of Cadet Jackson?"

"Where do you want me to start?" he asked. "I figure Dr. Griffin probably gave you the important details."

"He did," she replied. "But I want to get your impression on the proceedings. Tell me what happened, from when you first stepped into the room. Leave nothing out."

"Nothing?" he asked. There weren't many words in the English language that were both as specific and as vague as that one.

"Nothing," she repeated.

"Okay, then." McCoy slipped into his story, telling her about his arrival in the empty room, but leaving out the part about his temptation to peek under the sheet. That was a little too much of nothing in his opinion.

Under other circumstances, he might have glossed over the part about Dr. Peteque walking in, but since the captain had already interviewed her, he figured omitting it would be pointless. And possibly look suspicious. Once he got past that, he moved on to Dr. Griffin's arrival and the more salient information.

The captain was silent throughout his retelling of the morning's events. She nodded a few times, prodding him on. She even cracked a smile on one occasion when he'd made a lighthearted comment about the lack of sleep for cadets at Starfleet Medical to break the tension in the room. Otherwise, she was stone-faced and professional, not giving even the smallest hint if he was providing the information she wanted.

"And then Dr. Griffin sent me to his office till he told me to come here," McCoy concluded.

"So *you* were the one who discovered the rare disease was actually an intentional procedure?" It was the first thing Warde had said since McCoy started his monologue.

She hadn't said it in an accusatory manner, but he felt like he had to protect Dr. Griffin all the same. "The evidence was microscopic. Anyone could have missed it."

"But a follow-up examination would have probably revealed it?" she asked.

McCoy couldn't imagine that a follow-up would have been necessary. How many autopsies would be performed? "Only if the doctor knew what to look for. I'd never heard of this congenital insensitivity to pain. Without that information, I never would have found the evidence of micro-surgery."

"You've been a doctor for how long?" she asked.

"Few years."

"So the odds of you coming across this—"

"The odds of *anyone* coming across this are slim to beyond none," McCoy interrupted, his temper rising. He'd used his time in Griffin's office to research the disorder. It had been eradicated from Earth long before McCoy had been born. Captain Warde wasn't accusing him of any-thing, but somehow it felt like she was. The leading ques-tions. The innuendo in her tone. It felt like she was guiding him down a path he didn't want to go.

"Where would someone perform this kind of oper-ation?"

"How in the world should I know?" McCoy said. "With today's medical gadgetry, probably anywhere. This confer-ence room. Your office. Doubt you'd need some kind of medical facility."

"But you would need advanced equipment?"

McCoy had been so focused on the medicine behind what Cadet Jackson had suffered that he failed to examine it from the practical side. It was such a basic question he'd overlooked. "Of course," he replied.

"Of course, what?"

"This wasn't some fly-by-night thing," McCoy said. "This kind of surgery took special planning. And special instrumentation. Microsurgery of this type would be otherwise impossible. We're talking about a very precise operation on the nerve fibers. Especially considering it barely left any scarring behind."

"Which is why it was lucky you found the evidence."

"Exactly," he said, ignoring the suspicion in her tone. "Now, a doctor might be able to do that kind of surgery with a tri-laser connector, but I doubt it. You'd need something more specialized."

"Such as?"

McCoy searched his memory for information from his medical studies, and for the second time that day it failed him. "I don't know that the instrument exists."

CH.10.28
Combat Training

Kirk caught himself staring at the lithe body of Cadet Uhura as she ran through her warm-up routine. She wore the standard physical activities uniform all cadets wore, but she still managed to stand out among her classmates. It was another monochromatic red outfit, but in less restrictive design than the duty uniforms they typically wore. The material hugged her body, highlighting her form as she stretched.

Just looking at another girl wasn't cheating. He and Lynne hadn't even been on an official date yet. All the same, it somehow felt wrong when he caught Thanas staring as well.

"Nothing as enticing as the one who won't give you the time of day, huh, Kirk?" Thanas stepped onto the circular gray mat between them.

"You would know."

"What's that supposed to mean?"

"Haven't seen her holding on to your arm, have I?"

"Only have two arms." Thanas flexed his biceps. "They haven't been very lonely. And her partner over there kindly took up an arm when she escorted me to class."

Andros, Uhura's partner, was standing next to Uhura going through her own warm-up routines. She was a bundle of energy, jumping around to get the circulation flowing. There was something manic about her movements, which made it difficult to watch. It didn't match the contained grace of Cadet Uhura.

"Bet she won't even give you her first name." Kirk was taking his chances with that one. The odds weren't in his favor that she withheld that information from Thanas as she had with Kirk.

Thanas didn't respond, but the uncomfortable expression on his face said it all. Kirk wasn't sure if Andorians blushed, but there did seem to be a darker tint to the blue of his cheeks. Kirk felt a lot better knowing he wasn't the only one she'd blown off.

Kirk stepped onto the gray mat. It was cold under his bare feet, but that wasn't the real problem. The soft, pliant cushion gave a bit more bounce to his step than he'd anticipated.

He would have preferred to do this exercise on the gymnasium floor, but safety precautions had to be followed. In light of the cadet death that was just beginning to make the rounds in the gossip mill, he guessed that he could understand the instructor's need to take precautions.

Kirk bowed to Thanas, which earned him an echoing laugh in return. When he rose, he noted the silence around him. All eyes in the room had turned at the sound of Thanas's forced laughter. Now it was Kirk's turn to blush.

"Ancient Earth customs are out of place in Rigelian martial arts," Lieutenant Commander Bjorta announced to the class. He was using Kirk's slipup as a teaching example, not to embarrass him. At least that's what Kirk told himself so that he didn't lash out as his instructor.

He'd rather save his anger for Thanas.

"Rigelian hand-to-hand combat is more . . . indirect," Bjorta continued. "The moves are simple, concise, and work best when they come at an opponent without warning. There's nothing polite about Rigelian combat." The lieutenant commander put his hands on Uhura's shoulders. He guided her movements, circling with her fight partner. Bjorta waved to the other cadets, indicating that they should follow his lead.

Kirk waited for Thanas to make the first move. When the Andorian stepped left, Kirk stepped right. They circled the mat with their eyes locked on each other, ready to strike the moment their instructor gave the signal.

"Each move has a purpose," Bjorta continued, moving with Uhura as the cadets circled one another. "Step. Counterstep. Each blow should be focused on one of four spots on the body. Right flank. Neck. Knees. Lower back. Any other contact is either meant as a distraction or an utter waste of time."

The lieutenant commander moved off the mat he shared with Uhura and her partner, allowing them to circle freely on their own. "Remember the moves I showed you yesterday. The moves you were all supposed to practice last night. The entirety of Rigelian martial arts consists of those six basic steps. Now's the time to use them."

Confusion flashed through Kirk's mind. He could only remember five steps. He'd only practiced five moves.

Again, he focused on his breathing. It would be fine.

"Ready?" Bjorta said.

Five moves were all Kirk would need.

"Go!"

Thanas lashed out the moment Bjorta gave the command.

Kirk was ready for the move, and countered. Thanas's hand swiped through empty air. "Stealth," Kirk taunted. "It's not about a frontal— Agh!"

Thanas's fist pounded into Kirk's side.

"You talk too much," Thanas said with a giddy leer.

That was funny coming from the cadet who never shut up about himself, but Kirk chose not to prove him right by saying it. He focused on the fight instead. It was bad enough that he'd allowed Thanas to land the first blow.

Grunts and yells filled the room as the cadets went after one another. Kirk and Thanas continued to circle, staring each other down. This fight was going to be more psychological.

They both moved at once. Kirk kicked Thanas's weak spot at the knee. Thanas came down on Kirk's neck. They both made contact.

Pain flared down Kirk's spine.

Thanas's leg went out from under him.

He was back up before Kirk could capitalize on Thanas's weakened position. In Rigelian martial arts, the lower back was the sweet spot. Hit it just right, and you could incapacitate your opponent. It was almost impossible to reach it when the opponents circled the mat face-to-face, refusing to drop their guard.

Winners were declared all over the room, yet Kirk and his combatant had landed a total of only three blows so far between them.

It was time to get serious.

The two cadets struck again in unison.

Kirk smashed a hand into Thanas's flank, hitting the soft, fleshy spot beneath the rib cage. Thanas went for the same spot on Kirk, but missed, catching him in the gut. Kirk wasn't so sure it was accidental.

The onslaught did not stop. They exchanged blows in rapid succession, inflicting actual pain. It was supposed to be a sparring match. They were going for blood.

Lieutenant Commander Bjorta should have called them off, should have stopped things when it became clear that the sparring had moved to something personal.

He didn't.

The other cadets came over to watch.

Thanas got in another cheap shot to Kirk's gut. His body blocked the dirty move from Bjorta's view. If the instructor didn't see it, he couldn't call it.

"Lieutenant Commander Bjorta!" The voice was Uhura's. She was trying to get the instructor to intercede. No official call came.

The Andorian went in for a final blow. Kirk still had the wind knocked out of him. It was all Kirk could do to remain standing. One more strike would take him down.

Thanas pulled back.

Kirk kneed the Andorian in the soft spot between his legs, using a move as old as humanity itself. The Andorian doubled over, exposing his back. Kirk jumped up, landing an elbow in the sweet spot, flattening Thanas.

Nobody cheered. Several female cadets rushed to Thanas's aid. Uhura wasn't one of them, but her partner was.

The lieutenant commander was right up in Kirk's face. "What the hell was that?"

"Rigelian martial arts, sir," Kirk said with a cocky smile. "Element of surprise."

One of the girls, who was bending to help Thanas, laughed.

"That was not a sanctioned move, and you know it, plebe," Bjorta barked.

"True," Kirk replied. "But kicking him there allowed me to make the final shot that took him out. Just being practical, sir. Distraction."

"You are aware that Rigelians have multiple genders, are you not, plebe?"

"Yes," Kirk lied. He had no idea what the lieutenant commander was talking about. Or why. He was also getting annoyed by the "plebe" name-calling. Instructors didn't usually do that. The word was usually reserved for the upperclassmen to use. Bjorta calling him that was meant as a put-down. That was certain.

"So there's no guarantee that on a Rigelian, the move you pulled would even work," Bjorta said. "Hell, who's to say it would even work on an Andorian?"

The lieutenant commander didn't need to raise his voice any louder, but he did refocus his attention to the rest of the class. "Don't assume that just because your race has a particular weakness, *all* races share that weakness." He brought down his voice to a controlled level and looked right at Kirk again. "And don't assume you can keep pulling illegal moves and get away with it in my class, plebe. You've failed today."

Bjorta turned back to the class. "Resume starting

positions for round two," he ordered.

Kirk wanted to respond as the instructor stepped away, but he knew better.

"Low blow." Thanas groaned as he got to his feet, shaking off the female attention.

Kirk grit his teeth. "Don't act like you didn't throw in a few dirty shots."

"The difference is, I didn't get caught."

Kirk squared his shoulders, standing toe to toe with the Andorian. "Doesn't matter who got what. You're the one who ended up flat on the mat."

"Only because I knew enough to lay low when teacher was around," Thanas said. "I doubt you could hold your own against me when the faculty isn't paying attention."

Kirk held up his hands, beckoning for the opportunity. "Anytime."

Thanas checked to make sure no one would overhear. The other cadets had scattered. Even his closest admirer was off with Uhura, preparing for their next sparring match.

"There's a little get-together," Thanas said. "Tomorrow night. Midpoint on the Golden Gate Bridge. For cadets that really want to show their abilities."

"Sounds interesting," Kirk said. Actually, it sounded stupid, but he didn't want to be accused of backing down.

Thanas threw him a challenging glare. "It will be."

CH.11.28
Medical Emergency

Uhura checked the clock in the quad. Theoretically, she had enough time to swing by the mess hall and grab a snack on her way to Astrosciences. The cafeteria was on the way to that building. At the same time, she didn't want to risk being late. Today was the final review before a test, and she was hopelessly behind.

"Uhura, wait up!"

She glanced back and saw her combat training partner, Andros, chasing after her. Waiting was not an option if she wanted to grab some food, but she did slow down. Andros was running fast enough that she'd catch up in a matter of moments.

Uhura's stomach grumbled. She'd been so concerned about studying that she'd forgotten to eat anything during lunch, which was just stupid. She wasn't going to be able to focus on the review with an empty stomach. She'd never hear the instructor over the growling.

The sound of Andros's footsteps grew louder as she reached Uhura. "Hey, thanks for slowing down. I wanted to go over that last sparring match with you."

"So long as you don't mind keeping pace."

"No problem," she said, even though she was already out of breath, which was odd since she hadn't really run that far after Uhura. They'd also had a good cool-down period after their workout. Followed by plenty of time to change for the next class. Andros shouldn't have been breathing that heavily.

"So, that last match," Andros said.

"Yeah. Sorry about that. I didn't mean to take your legs out from under you like I did." Actually, Uhura had meant to do exactly that. She just hadn't expected Andros to drop so hard.

Andros had won most of their matches, but not because she was better skilled in Rigelian martial arts. If anything, she still had a lot to learn. Her form was awful. Only about half her moves were sanctioned. She'd mainly won most matches by wearing Uhura down. Andros had been all over the mat, a flurry of arms and legs moving in every direction. Uhura only managed to win the final round by landing a lucky kick.

Andros should have dropped to the ground, but she was flailing so hard, trying to keep on her feet, that she sent herself flying backward off the mat and onto the hard floor. Uhura could still hear the sound of her head making contact with the ground. It echoed in Uhura's memory.

"So what did I do wrong?" Andros asked. "That let you take me down like that?"

"Honestly, I don't know," Uhura replied. "You were moving so fast, it was kind of hard to tell."

"Got a lot of pent-up energy."

"It would seem."

Andros huffed even harder. Sweat dripped from her hair even though it was a pleasant fall day. They were walking at a brisk pace, but not that brisk. Uhura slowed some more, not wanting to exhaust her partner.

"Actually . . . you mind if we stop for a sec? Let me catch my breath?"

Uhura did mind, but she didn't want to say it. Andros clearly needed to stop. Her breathing was growing more rapid. Her face paled.

"Are you okay?" Uhura asked.

"Fine," Andros replied. It came out in a squeak.

"Maybe you should sit down."

"Good idea."

Uhura started to lead her to the nearest bench, but Andros couldn't make it. She collapsed onto the grass. "Andros?" Uhura dropped beside her.

Andros waved her off. "I'm fine," she said between panting breaths. "Okay."

"I think we should take you to Medical."

"No! Just need . . ." The cadet's pupils rolled up into her head, exposing the whites of her eyes. Her body listed to the side.

"Andros! Andros! Karin!"

A small crowd formed around them as Uhura pulled out her communicator. She flipped it open. "Cadet Uhura to Academy Medical. We need an emergency medical team on the quad. I've got—"

Andros started convulsing. Her mouth foamed.

"Scratch that. We need an emergency medical transport from this location. Now!"

Within moments she experienced the odd sensation of the world around her shifting. Her body transformed into a matter stream that was transported across campus. In the blink of an eye, the grass and sky were replaced by the soothing white/blue walls of the emergency sickbay at Starfleet Medical. The concerned cadets who had gathered to watch on the quad were now a pair of trained professionals who, hopefully, knew what to do. Uhura was still in her crouched position. She rose to take in the scene.

Andros was lying on a biobed on an emergency medical transport pad. She'd stopped convulsing. Her pupils had returned, but they stared at the ceiling. Empty of life.

Dr. McCoy rushed to her side. "What have we got?" he asked with a Southern drawl as he grabbed a medical tricorder off the exam table beside them. He pulled the cylindrical scanner from the boxy device and ran the instrument over Andros's body.

"She collapsed out on the quad," Uhura explained. "We'd just come from Combat Training. She fell and hit her head in class."

McCoy ran the scanner over Andros's head. He checked the readout on the device. "No sign of concussion. What else?"

"She was out of breath. Panting. And sweating." Uhura thought back to what had happened. She mentally catalogued every symptom she'd witnessed. "Her eyes rolled back into her head when she passed out."

He continued to run the scanner over her body. His brow furrowed when he read something off the screen. Then he reexamined the same spot. His response was the same.

"Is something wrong?"

He looked at her like he was almost surprised she was still there. "No," he said. "You can . . . um . . . you can get back to class."

If McCoy thought he was being reassuring, he had to learn a bit about bedside manners. "What is it? What's wrong with her?" Uhura asked.

McCoy motioned to the nurse who took Uhura by the shoulder and gently guided her away from the exam area.

"The doctor's going to run a few tests," he said. "Don't want to give a premature diagnosis. Won't know anything for a while. You should get to class. Leave your name on the PADD, and we'll update you when we know something."

The nurse took a nearby PADD from the counter and handed it to her. Uhura couldn't fill it out yet. "I should wait here. She might want a familiar face when she wakes."

"She might be out for a while." He skillfully escorted her into the hall without her even realizing it. The sickbay door shut behind them.

"I should wait," Uhura said, though she wasn't sure why. She and Andros had only talked to each other in class. But something was going on, something the doctor didn't want her to see.

In light of Thanas's news about Jackson, this worried Uhura. The fears didn't ease when an older doctor—an instructor—rushed past her and went into the room. "What's going on?" she asked the nurse.

"You got me." His tranquil mask slipped a little. The other doctor's sudden arrival had surprised him as well. "But I'd better get back. They might need me. Leave your info on the PADD."

He handed her the device and turned away without another word. Uhura had more questions, but she didn't want to keep the nurse from his duties. Andros's health was the more important factor, not her curiosity.

That changed dramatically when she saw that the door to sickbay refused to open for the nurse. He'd been locked out. He now looked just as confused as Uhura felt.

· · ✢ ∶ ✦ · ✦ ·· ·

"Report," Dr. Griffin commanded once he'd secured the door to sickbay.

McCoy handed over the medical tricorder. "Patient just came in. Collapsed in the quad. Her friend reported that she'd hit her head in class. I don't think that's the problem."

Dr. Griffin took in the pale body before them. Her chest rose and fell at a rapid rate. Shivers wracked her body. Though she was unconscious, she was far from immobile. "I can see that," he said. "Walk me through it."

"Her metabolism is . . . well, it's supercharged. Her body is processing energy at an incredible rate, throwing her cells out of homeostasis."

"She's expending more energy than she's taking in," Dr. Griffin agreed.

"For her to maintain those numbers, she'd have to be eating constantly."

"It's good that you called me," Griffin said. "This is an unusual case. We should treat her—"

McCoy jumped in. "I've already administered treatment," he said. "While you were on the way here. That's not why I called you."

"I suspected as much," Griffin said. "Let me guess. This is not a natural occurrence."

"The enzymes in her body have been altered."

"Drugs?"

McCoy nodded. First illegal surgery, now illegal drugs. The kind that wouldn't be picked up in a routine drug screening. This did not look good. "For her to maintain these levels, she'd need to be on special medication. Then she'd need a proper amount of food to fuel the body."

"As if cadets didn't have enough trouble struggling to keep up with the Academy schedule. The rigors of keeping up with this regimen . . . It's no surprise she'd be here."

McCoy administered a hypospray filled with a sedative. The body stopped shivering. Her eyes closed.

"This has to stop," Griffin said. It was barely a whisper.

"Should we report this to Captain Warde?"

The question shook Griffin out of his thoughts. "I want to go over these scans first."

"Figured you might." McCoy stepped aside from the cadet to let the doctor get closer.

"Thank you for alerting me," Griffin said. "Take the rest of the afternoon off. And you should probably expect a visit from Captain Warde."

Actually, McCoy was expecting to see his patient through her treatment. "Sir? Are you telling me to leave?"

Griffin looked up at McCoy as if the question were

unexpected. "I'm telling you that you're dismissed."

"But, sir, I'm the physician on record."

"Yes, and you've done a fine job, McCoy," he said. "But while this cadet rests off whatever is going on in her body, it would be best for us if another cadet was not involved in the treatment. We need to make sure that she has the best care available."

McCoy was offended. "But, sir—"

"I'm speaking of the official records," Griffin quickly added. "For the *record*, she needs senior level treatment. You and I both know that you're a good doctor, but there's no room for screwups here. The administration will not abide a cadet treating such an important case, if this does turn out to be linked to the death of Cadet Jackson."

McCoy wanted to say something, but he wasn't sure he could control his tongue. It wasn't fair to the patient to take him off the case just because of bureaucracy. He was the attending physician. He should be the one to monitor her progress.

"I assure you, the patient is in capable hands," Griffin said lightly.

"It's not that," McCoy said. "It's just—" But he wasn't sure what it was. Probably ego. He'd never been taken off a case before. Sure, there were extenuating circum-stances, but that didn't change anything. He was being told he could no longer treat a patient. And there was nothing he could do about it.

"If you'll excuse me, I need to get to work."

"Yes, sir," McCoy said.

He took a final look at the sedated patient. She seemed so peaceful there, at rest. No evidence of the war that raged in her body.

Griffin must have noticed that the cadet had yet to move. "And talk to the nurse," he added. "Need to make sure nothing about this cadet goes beyond this room."

"Will do," McCoy said. Then he added, "Sir."

CH.12.28
Truth and Rumors

Hours later Kirk was still feeling the anger from his combat training run-in with Thanas and Lieutenant Commander Bjorta. The class was all he could think about as he shed his uniform and changed into civilian clothes.

It was bad enough that Lieutenant Commander Bjorta had berated Kirk in front of the whole class, but that smug smile on Thanas's face during the entire time really pushed him over the edge. What did he have to be so cocky about? He'd been the one writhing on the ground. And he didn't fare much better in the later rounds. Thanas had been more concerned with grandstanding than fighting.

So much for the winner of the survival course.

Okay, the low blow wasn't exactly standard Starfleet maneuver, but it got the job done. In a real fight, properly sanctioned moves weren't important. All that mattered was who was on their feet at the end.

In class, more often than not, the one left standing had been Kirk.

He checked his cocky smile in the mirror and liked what he saw. It was a nice change to be out of the standard cadet uniform and in casual clothes. Felt like it was the first time he'd been out of uniform in weeks. Come to think of it, it was. When he wasn't in uniform, he was usually in bed. Sometimes he was in bed in uniform. The Academy training was that intense.

Kirk still hadn't decided whether or not this was the place for him. Maybe his date with Lynne tonight would cinch things. She was the best reason he could think of to stick around. His smile grew with thoughts of her. He turned from his mirror and made for the door to his quarters, nearly smacking into McCoy as he stepped into the hall. "Bones!"

"You planning on calling me that the rest of my life?" McCoy shot back.

Kirk paused for a moment, surprised by the anger from his friend. Bones tended to be on the cantankerous side, but this was different. In the silent beat that followed, Kirk considered McCoy's question. "I like it, *Bones*. I think it'll stick."

McCoy cracked a smile. "You do realize I'm going to get you back for that someday."

"As long as it's not today," Kirk said. "Don't know if I want to go up against you in this mood. What's up?"

McCoy glanced down the hall. It was loaded with

cadets heading to and from their late classes, the mess hall, or out for the evening. The campus was a constant buzz of activity. The dorms were no exception. He nodded toward Kirk's room. "Got a minute?"

Kirk checked the time. He was already running late. "Not really. Walk with me into town?"

McCoy shrugged. "That might help blow off some steam."

Kirk had never seen his friend *this* angry before. He stepped out into the hall, and they went toward the lift that would take them down to ground level.

"What're you all gussied up for?" McCoy asked, obviously avoiding the subject that had put him in a mood until they were out of the building.

Kirk hadn't considered himself "all gussied up." In fact, he'd chosen the worn jeans and vintage T-shirt specifically because he wanted to look casual. He also didn't think the leather bomber jacket would count as gussying up either. Not that that was a term *he'd* ever use at any rate. "Finally going on that date with Monica."

"About time," McCoy said. "Where you taking her?"

"I'm not," Kirk said. "She's taking me."

McCoy raised an eyebrow. "Is she now? Don't see her picking you up. Isn't that standard operating procedure for a date? The *dater* picks up the *datee* and takes her . . . um . . . *him* out on the town?"

"Funny," Kirk said as they exited through the back of

the building. "She sent me a message. I'm meeting her someplace on Marina. Wouldn't tell me what it was."

"Sounds mysterious."

"I could use a little mystery in my life," Kirk said as they crossed the quad. He was looking forward to exploring the city. He'd hardly been off campus since he got there. So much of his life had been spent trapped in Riverside, Iowa, that he'd planned to hit the city as often as he could while he was at the Academy. But with the exception of a few class assignments that took him around town, he'd hardly scratched the surface of what San Francisco had to offer.

"Well, I could use a little less mystery," McCoy muttered softly. He ignored Kirk's "tell me more" look.

San Francisco had its fair share of Starfleet officers and cadets strolling through the city. It wasn't like they'd be safe to talk freely without being overheard. But there was something that just felt different about being outside the Academy. A freedom that didn't exist on the perfectly manicured grounds of the campus. Once they were out on the streets of San Francisco, McCoy finally opened up about what was bothering him. "Some days I wish I'd stayed a country doc."

"Nothing here could ever be so bad that it would ever get me to miss home."

McCoy looked over his friend. "That's 'cause you were made for the adventure of space."

Kirk thought back to being disciplined in combat training. "I'm not so sure Starfleet understands the concept of adventure."

McCoy let out a derisive snort. "I think they understand it too much."

"All these stupid rules and regulations."

"Are there for a reason," McCoy said as they started across a major thoroughfare. Rows of hovervehicles lined up beside them, their electric engines humming quietly while the drivers waited for the light to change so they could continue on their way. "And even then, they don't cover everything a stupid kid will do. Not nearly."

Kirk suspected they'd touched on the topic at hand. "Is that what your mood is about? The rumors of that cadet who died?"

McCoy stopped short in the crosswalk, clearly surprised. "How'd you hear about that?"

Kirk kept walking. The light was about to change. "You really think news like that wouldn't spread?"

"Kind of thought it might take a bit longer," McCoy replied as he fell in beside his friend. "The administration's working overtime to hush it up."

"You know what happened?" Kirk asked. He wasn't one for idle gossip, but he was genuinely curious. If something dangerous was going on at the Academy, it was only right to alert the cadets. Especially seeing how someone like

Thanas was already keeping the student body informed.

"Know more than I want to." McCoy sighed. "I was assigned to the autopsy."

That was the last thing Kirk expected to hear. "They let a student in on the autopsy? I thought they'd want to keep tight control on that."

"I was surprised too, at first. Doubt that they expected us to find what we discovered. Probably didn't expect what happened this afternoon either."

Just then Kirk saw an officer strolling in their direction and turned down a side street. McCoy picked up on what was happening and followed. It was quieter off the main drag, so they didn't have to keep their voices up to compete with traffic. Kirk knew they were being paranoid, but it was best to play it safe. "What happened?" he asked in a low voice.

"You can't tell anyone," McCoy said. "Not even your girlfriend."

"She's not my girlfriend. Not yet, anyway."

"Whatever she is, this has to stay between us."

"No problem," Kirk said. He never had any issue with keeping things to himself before. Heck, he'd spent most of his life bottling things up inside. Random gossip about some near total stranger wasn't that big a deal.

"Okay, so, Jackson, he was . . . how shall I say this?" McCoy stalled, like he was trying to figure out the best way to explain it. "Let me keep this simple."

"I've been told I'm kind of a smart guy," Kirk joked. "Might surprise you what I can figure out."

"Don't think they were calling you a smart *guy*," McCoy replied. "But I'm not sure I entirely understand what's going on myself."

They walked the next half block in silence while McCoy organized his thoughts. Once they turned out of the side street, Kirk saw that they were almost at the address Lynne had given him. It was a tiny shack of a restaurant with a beach theme called Suraya Bay. McCoy had better get talking soon or else they'd have no choice but to share the news with his date.

McCoy stopped when they saw the restaurant a half block away. "Cadet Jackson died from the cumulative wounds he sustained over these first few weeks—maybe months—of training."

"No wonder they want to keep this quiet," Kirk said. He'd often thought the training had been a bit on the intense side. Not for himself, but for some of the others. He never imagined the intensity was dangerous, but now that he heard it had taken a life, he wasn't entirely surprised.

"That's not the big news," McCoy said. "Jackson underwent some kind of procedure. An operation that would keep him from feeling pain. We think he did it to perform better in his training."

"No pain, no gain," Kirk said lightly. Kirk knew it wasn't

the time for jokes, but it sort of came out on its own. He was glad that McCoy trusted him enough to confide this in him, but he was also worried what would happen if anyone found out what he knew. This kind of thing was a serious breach to the all-important honor code. A code that, so far, Kirk had only known the *cadets* were forced to follow. It had to be against some code for the administration to keep this kind of information from the student body. That didn't seem very honorable.

He remembered back to Jackson falling off the cliff face. He'd jumped back up without a wince, yet Kirk had thought at the time that the kid had to be hurting. At least this explained his reaction. He probably did some real damage to his body in that fall.

"That's the damn problem. Without that pain, he didn't know how badly his body had been suffering. He didn't have to die."

"I get why he might've done it, though," Kirk said.

"Care to explain it to me?"

"This place messes with your head," Kirk said. "I pulled a sucker punch on a guy in class earlier. I'll be the first to admit, I'm not above a sucker punch every now and then, but in class? I was showing off. We all do it every day."

"That would explain the other patient I saw today. They probably didn't expect what I'd see."

"Which was?"

"First-year cadet," McCoy explained. "Came in unconscious. Result of a high metabolism. Uhura brought her in."

"Really? That's interesting, but what's it got to do with Jackson?"

"I'm getting to it," McCoy said. "She was taking something to elevate her metabolism. Probably to keep her body weight down. Bring her energy level up. Help her get through training."

"Is she . . . ?"

"Alive," McCoy said. "But sedated last I heard. She won't be talking for a while. Got to give her body a chance to adjust."

"Sounds like an epidemic."

"Two does not make an epidemic," McCoy said. "Not usually. But there's something about this. Yeah. I don't think this thing is contained."

"What's the administration doing about it?"

"They've got some hot-shot captain on it," McCoy said. "Warde. Asks all kinds of questions. Mostly good questions, but that's not the problem. Once I diagnosed the second cadet this afternoon, I was shut out completely. She's *my* patient. I said as much when Warde came to see me later for more questions."

"Bet she didn't care."

"Not one iota," he said. "Claimed it was standard procedure. But I think something funny's going on. I may be wrong, but I think the Academy will try to cover this thing up too."

CH.13.28
An Uninvited Guest

Spock did not relish a return to the cadet dorms. He had suffered the indignity of shared living space with hundreds of other young students during his earlier years at the Academy. When he'd enrolled at Starfleet Academy, he hadn't anticipated how difficult it would be to reside among a mix of emotional races all day and night.

It was one thing to attend classes with the other students. It was quite another to live among them as they had their secretive parties and emotional mood swings. His first-year roommate had been a particularly obnoxious human, more concerned with celebrating the fact that he was accepted to the Academy than focusing on what it meant to be a student. He washed out midway through the first year.

Spock had found that a surprising number of cadets had not yet reached the maturity level to be Starfleet officers, which was the point of the Academy training program.

Spock much preferred the faculty living quarters. That situation was not perfect either, but it was preferable to the environment in which he currently found himself.

A pair of young human males, dripping wet from the showers and dressed in nothing but towels, bumped into him as they rushed past. The half-hearted apologies they offered as they continued down the hall did not make up for getting water all over the unfolded boxes he was carrying. Spock considered calling them back, but he shuddered to think how they might offer to dry the boxes. He merely wiped the surface of the box that had gotten the most wet with his sleeve.

Spock was pleased when he finally reached his destination. He no longer had to navigate the halls—at least not until his departure.

"What?" a voice yelled out when the door chimed, announcing Spock's presence. It was not the standard expected reply when one was at the door. He could very easily have been a senior officer waiting for admittance. Even a lower grade officer like himself was due more respect than a holler.

Spock did not reply to the yelled question. It was unseemly to shout through a door, particularly since the occupant would surely open it upon hearing the sound of a second chime.

His assumption was correct. The door opened a moment

later. Spock registered the expression on the Andorian cadet's face as annoyance. He suspected it had something to do with the young woman seated on the edge of the cadet's bed. They were both in full uniform, signifying that Spock had not interrupted anything. At least, not yet.

"Cadet Thanas." Spock nodded in greeting. They had never met previously, but Spock recognized the cadet from the image in his file.

"Yeah?" The cadet's body language suggested that Spock had little time to gain entrance to his quarters. He took one step forward, blocking the door sensor to ensure that it would not suddenly shut.

"Please allow me to express my regrets for your loss," Spock said. He'd learned that opening on a personal level usually help set an emotional race at ease.

"Loss?" Thanas asked. He looked back at the young woman on his bed, who was casually going through the things on his nightstand. "Oh, you mean Jackie. We weren't exactly close. Not so much the loss of a roommate as the gain of a single suite. Know what I'm saying?"

Apparently emotional concerns were not the case with this particular individual. The way he'd taken Jackson's name and turned it into a juvenile moniker also spoke volumes.

Spock moved on, taking another step into the door-way. He had now situated himself inside the room. Thanas looked as though he wanted to say something, but knew enough not to challenge a superior. "I've been asked to collect Cadet Jackson's personal effects to return to his family."

"Now?"

Spock leaned the unfolded boxes against the interior wall as a statement of his intent to proceed. Captain Warde had suggested this subterfuge as a means of getting Spock "in the door," as she had said. She had meant it figuratively, but it worked equally as well in the literal sense.

Thanas leaned uncomfortably close to Spock and whispered, "I'm kind of in the middle of something."

Spock had seen non-Vulcans grieve before. It was, occasionally, a messy affair. Oftentimes outsiders would dismiss the Vulcan grieving process for being uncaring, but that could not be further from the truth. Vulcans grieved deeply, though they worked to ensure that the emotions did not show. This was the first time Spock ever witnessed someone who clearly experienced no remorse for the loss of a person with whom he had been living for months.

"I am certain you understand that Cadet Jackson's family is in pain," Spock said. "Having their son's belongings around them might ease their suffering." That was another one of Captain Warde's suggestions. Spock could not fathom how any person could take solace from inanimate objects.

The ruse seemed to do the trick, if Thanas's reaction was any indication. He turned to his female companion and asked, "We can go to your dorm room, right?"

"I was hoping to have your assistance," Spock quickly added. The ruse was useless if Thanas left.

Thanas let out a snort of a laugh, and ignored Spock. "Well?" he asked his friend.

She got up off the bed, not looking very disappointed so far as Spock could tell. "Can't," she said. "My roommate is hosting a study group. Maybe tomorrow night."

Thanas put out his arm, blocking the doorway before she could leave the room. "I may have plans tomorrow night," he warned.

"Then it will be your loss," she said. Even Spock recognized a good exit line as she slipped under the cadet's arm, and they both watched her saunter through the door and down the hall.

Thanas eyed Spock with uncontained hostility. "You have no idea what you just interrupted."

Spock chose not to challenge that assertion. It wasn't difficult to imagine what Thanas had been hoping would occur.

Spock started to assemble the boxes so they could be filled, unfolding them into their more useful position. "It will be helpful for you to remain here so that I do not accidentally pack any of your belongings."

Thanas dropped down on his bed without offering a hand. "No worries there." He pointed to the opposite side of the room. "Everything over there was Jackie's. Everything over here is mine. Our stuff didn't really comingle."

Once the boxes were assembled, Spock made a visual inspection of the room. Thanas was correct in his assessment of his personal quarters. The room was well delineated between his side of the room and Jackson's.

The Andorian was lying in bed in the midst of the most cluttered space Spock had ever witnessed. The room would never pass inspection. It also said much about the cadet's quality as a romantic partner, considering he did not respect his former guest enough to straighten up before he invited her in.

Cadet Jackson's side of the room was immaculate. A textbook case of the proper care for one's quarters. This resembled more of life on a starship, where cleanliness and order were the ideal. The mess that Thanas lived in could be dangerous onboard a starship. Malfunctioning environmental controls had been known to disrupt the artificial gravity, which, in an extreme case, could turn any number of the items surrounding the cadet into projectiles. Good thing they were still planet bound.

Spock was envious of one element of the living situation. His roommate during his first year did not respect personal boundaries. He was constantly borrowing

Spock's property without asking. Spock still suspected that his former roommate had left with a number of his personal belongings when he was discharged. Cadets Thanas and Jackson clearly kept their items separate. That would make Spock's task easier.

Captain Warde had already been through the room earlier, looking for anything that could be considered evidence. Still, she had instructed him to take note of anything she may have missed as he catalogued the remaining items. She seemed to indicate that Spock could learn a lot about the cadet from examining his belongings. He did not see how that would be relevant to the investigation, but tried to keep an open mind.

He began with the cadet's desk. It was unlikely there was any information on the illegal surgery the cadet undertook, but it seemed the logical place to start. As he collected Jackson's items, Spock tried to engage the boy's roommate in one of his least favorite past times: small talk.

"You said earlier that you disliked your roommate?" Spock asked, beginning his informal questioning.

"What? No. Jackie was okay," Thanas said. "Just didn't have much in common. "Didn't like him. Didn't *not* like him."

Spock had a difficult time following that line of reasoning. "So you weren't enemies?"

Thanas picked a purple tennis ball off the ground and tossed into the air above him as he lay in his bed. "Didn't have anything to be enemies about. We weren't exactly in the same league."

"You did not consider Cadet Jackson a peer?"

"Well, yeah," Thanas said. "He was a *peer*. Wasn't much competition."

"Starfleet Academy is a serious educational institution," Spock reminded him. "It is not a competition."

"Guess you didn't hear I came in first during the Desert Survival Course." There was a momentary silence. "Oh, that's right, the teachers act like that doesn't happen. Well, I figured word spread."

"From what I understand, Cadet Jackson finished in a respectable place himself," Spock said. He'd read it in the cadet's file. Very little occurred at the Academy without the administration's knowledge of it. That held true for many of the unsanctioned events.

"Only respectable place in that race is first," Thanas said. The tennis ball made another high arc, almost touching the ceiling. "Maybe Vulcans don't get that whole competitive thing. Don't care much about winners. Or losers."

"Were you concerned about Cadet Jackson outperforming you?"

"Already said we weren't in the same league," Thanas repeated.

"What about Cadet Andros?"

Thanas trapped the tennis ball in his hands and turned to glare at Spock. "What about her?"

"It is my understanding that you are in a relationship."

"Did she tell you that? No. We went out a couple times. Had some fun. What do you care? You interested in her?" He looked Spock over. "Doubt she'd go for you."

Spock was almost offended that Thanas would think that comment would offend him. "I was just . . . surprised that you would be romancing another young woman when Cadet Andros lies unconscious in a medical bay."

This finally got the Andorian's attention. "Seriously? Anything I should be worried about? Nothing contagious, I hope."

Again, Spock was caught off guard by the lack of concern in his voice. Andorians weren't the most emotional of races, but they had no problem expressing themselves. "No. She is experiencing a different type of ailment."

"Good to know." Thanas leaned back and resumed throwing the tennis ball into the air.

"Interesting though that both your roommate and your . . . casual partner would be struck with medical conditions in the same twenty-four-hour period."

The ball stopped again. "I don't think I like what you're suggesting."

"I was merely commenting on the statistical—"

Thanas rose from his bed. "I don't like your statistics, either."

"I assure you," Spock said, "I meant no offense."

Thanas grabbed the box Spock was holding. "Know what? I think I'd rather pack up Jackie's stuff for him. Show some respect for his family. You can go."

Spock was not done with his questioning. "The job will go faster if both of us perform the task."

"That's okay," Thanas insisted. "I'm good here."

Spock realized that he had offended the cadet. Even if he managed to convince Thanas to allow him to stay, he doubted that any useful information would be forthcoming. Spock gave him a nod of thanks and left the room, mentally berating himself for failing in his mission to obtain any answers for the investigation.

CH.14.28
Sunset

Lynne had chosen a table out on the deck, with a spectacular view of water stretching out across the bay. The table kept with the intentionally tacky beach theme. It was painted to look like it had been built from driftwood. The chairs were modeled after canvas beach chairs. But it was the grass hut in the middle of each table that was the weirdest element by far. Kirk couldn't figure out what purpose it served, other than as a freakish centerpiece.

They sat beside each other in chairs facing the gorgeous vista. The sun was setting off to their left. The fading glow made for a nice reflection in the water off the north-facing shore. A chill breeze drifted inland, but heat lamps—and his proximity to Lynne—kept Kirk warm.

He didn't want McCoy's story to get in the way of the date, but it was hard to put aside what his friend had said. It seemed tasteless to think of relaxing with Lynne when Jackson's body was lying in the morgue and another cadet was fighting whatever it was she had over at Starfleet Medical.

"Someone's deep in thought," Lynne said, pulling him back into the moment.

"No," he said. "I'm just the strong, silent type."

"Too bad I like them weak and mouthy," she replied.

Her comment brought his thoughts right back to Jackson. It was horrible to think that way of the dead. Jackson wasn't weak. Just misguided. Kirk could understand the pressure the kid was under. He'd been feeling it enough himself. But he'd never understand going to such crazy lengths.

He felt Lynne's hand on his. "Tell me what's wrong."

It wasn't that she was overly perceptive. It would have been hard for anyone to miss that something was weighing on him. "It's nothing, really," Kirk said. "Now, what do you have planned for us tonight."

"That's a surprise," Lynne replied with a cryptic smile. She tapped some commands into the computer screen built into the driftwood table. The mix of modern technology and throwback furniture was weird, but Kirk didn't comment on the aesthetic. He was too busy trying to peek over Lynne's shoulder. She'd leaned her body so that Kirk couldn't see what she was ordering.

"I take it whatever you're ordering is a surprise as well?"

Lynne's response was a broader smile that brightened

her entire face, with a crinkled nose, and a twinkle in her eyes. The twinkle was more the reflection of light off the water, but Kirk enjoyed it all the same. "I'm full of surprises," she said.

As if punctuating her comment, a pair of colorful drinks appeared beneath the grass shack centerpiece. Kirk pulled the drinks from under the canopy. "You've got to be kidding," he said, genuinely impressed.

It wasn't magic. It was a tiny transporter built into the table and disguised to match the theme. Now that Kirk was paying more attention, he saw the painted transporter pad built into the fake driftwood.

He'd heard that a restaurant in San Francisco had adapted transporter technology to use for commercial purposes. Obviously this was the place. It seemed like a waste to him. Federation starships were equipped with transporters to send people and cargo across distances in the blink of an eye, not to save a restaurant from having to hire waiters.

But then he took a sip from the icy orange and red mixed beverage and forgot all about those concerns. The drink was delicious. A burst of mango and tropical fruits was only the initial experience as he took his first taste. There was the refreshing sensation of ice cold liquid going down his throat, gradually warming as it went on its journey. When he put his glass down, he was even more surprised to see that the drink was suddenly a mix of blue and green.

Lynne smiled when she saw the confused expression on Kirk's face. "It's called a Risian Rainbow. Every sip promises a new experience."

Another swallow revealed the drink now had the odd pairing of apple and blueberry. Kirk didn't like that as much as the first sip, but the now purple and yellow drink suggested a new sensation was forthcoming. "Interesting."

"You don't like it?"

"It is a little froufrou for me," he said, playing up the tough guy image he'd honed through years of practice. "I don't usually do drinks that come with umbrellas. Or in pastels."

"This is one of the healthiest drinks in the galaxy," she explained.

"Even worse," Kirk joked.

"Thought it would be good to get some vitamins in you if you plan to keep up with me tonight."

Lynne's words made his body temperature rise quite a few degrees, but Kirk tried to play it cool. He took a long chug of his frozen drink, risking brain freeze to show her that he was up for whatever she had planned.

He was somewhat relieved when Lynne pulled the glass from his lips before he finished it. "Okay, okay, you've made your point," she said, laughing.

He put the nearly empty glass back on the table. "I'm ready to go when you are."

Lynne ran her finger around the rim of her still mostly full drink. As her finger passed, the liquid changed color along the top edges. "Patience. I thought we could relax a bit first. Actually talk about something other than our classes. We've barely had any real conversations since we met."

"Sometimes silence is a virtue."

"Sometimes silence is overrated," she said as they fell into a comfortable, quiet moment together. Kirk was never big on the deep soul-searching conversations. Those usually just wound up with him talking about things he didn't want to discuss. This silent moment with Lynne was perfect as far as he was concerned.

But it didn't last nearly as long as Kirk had hoped.

"What brought you to Starfleet?" Lynne asked, bringing up the one subject he most did not want to discuss.

"An overcrowded shuttle," Kirk replied. It was a snotty response, but it was the only one he had. Captain Pike's challenge for Kirk to live up to his father's legacy was certainly a part of it. But he still wasn't sure what ultimately convinced him to join the Academy. And he definitely wasn't ready to share those feelings with anyone. Not yet, anyway. "What about you?"

He'd expected Lynne to respond with a joke, but she

was deadly serious when she said, "My application was filled out on my first day of elementary school."

"Parents wanted it, huh?" Kirk said. "I get that."

She let out an unrestrained bark of laughter. "Not even close. Joining Starfleet was the last thing my parents wanted for me."

Kirk leaned closer. "You've got my attention."

Lynne took a long drink from her glass as she gathered her thoughts. They both watched the Risian Rainbow change color. Kirk wasn't going to push her. If he didn't want to talk about his reasons, she certainly didn't have to share hers. Even though she was the one who asked the question in the first place. "My granddad was lost on one of the early deep space missions."

"I'm sorry," Kirk said. Obviously, he knew how that felt. She was probably under the same pressure he was to live up to someone who had come before.

"Not like your dad," she quickly added. "His ship was literally lost. The *Coronado*. Failed to make contact three months after leaving space dock. Never heard from again. Just gone. No explanation."

Kirk thought that might be worse than what he'd been through. At least he knew his dad was dead. Lynne still had hope for her granddad, unlikely though it was. "So you joined Starfleet hoping you could find him one day?"

"I'm not that big a dreamer," she replied. "Space is a big

place. I don't expect I'll ever know that answer."

The conversation took another pause as they watched the last of the fading sunlight on the water. Tacky tiki lights blinked on around them, and torches flared to life.

Lynne took another sip from her drink, which changed to a melancholy blue to match her mood. "Growing up not knowing my granddad . . . I did all I could to find out about him. Made me feel closer to him even though we never met."

Kirk nodded. "Big hero?"

Lynne smiled. "You're really bad at this. Why don't you let me tell the story on my own?"

Kirk sipped from what remained of his ever-changing drink, and waved her on.

"He was still an ensign when the ship was lost. Dad was about ten, living on Earth with Grandma when they got the news. Granddad was only a blip in Starfleet records."

Kirk wanted to ask her how she'd researched him, but knew he'd only get a smart response again. He took another sip as the rest of his drink shifted to an ominous black.

"I found his journals one day when I was staying with Grandma—my parents were vacationing on some planet," she said. "I had the actual journals that he'd written by hand. Dozens of them from high school, through his time at the Academy, to his first posting on a starship. It was the find of my life. Nothing else mattered to me after that."

Kirk hadn't seen an actual book in a while. He wasn't much of a reader, but what he did read was always on a PADD. He could imagine how it affected Lynne to be able to read her grandfather's handwriting, to touch the pages that he'd touched.

"Granddad didn't know anyone when he applied to the Academy," she explained. "He didn't have some officer writing him a recommendation. No recruiter came to town to seek him out. His grades were never great. He wasn't a star in school. He just contacted a recruiter and made his case."

She wasn't speaking directly about Kirk, but she could have been. Sure, she knew about his dad, but the rest of it wasn't exactly common knowledge. As far as he knew, Lynne was totally unaware that his path randomly crossed with the recruiter in a bar one night.

"They let him in, naturally," she said. "Weren't as picky back then. Not like it is today."

Kirk wondered what the Academy was like "back then" when space was still an adventure, not a political minefield. Back when they were still coming up with all those rules and regulations.

"Every day he wrote in his journal about how he struggled in his training," she continued. "How hard it was for him to pass the tests. To excel on the field. And this was in the early days of Starfleet. Nothing compared to what they expect from students today. I doubt he would have made it one week in our class."

Kirk's thoughts went to Cadet Jackson, lying dead in the morgue at Starfleet Medical. Maybe he would have made it through training back in the days Lynne's granddad was at the Academy. Or maybe he just wasn't cut out for this lifestyle after all.

"When I read those pages, I promised myself that I wasn't going to be a blip on the radar, only to disappear along with my ship. I started training right after I finished the first of his journals. Studying up on starships. Learning combat and flight procedures. Taking in all I could."

"And here you are," Kirk said, "finished in the top three in the Desert Survival Course."

"Don't rub it in," Lynne suddenly snapped.

The reaction caught Kirk off guard. "It was a compliment."

"I know, I know," she said, somewhat apologetically. "It's just hard for me to take it as one. Thanas gets to me with his arrogance and his fan club and his—"

Kirk moved closer. "*You've* got a fan club."

"Thanks," she said, but was still discouraged. "But there's something about Thanas. He makes it all look so easy. I don't trust him."

"Neither do I. But I don't want to waste our time together talking about Thanas or the Academy or anything like that." Kirk downed the last of his drink. "I'm ready for this mystery date to start."

They both looked down at Lynne's drink. The glass was only half empty. Or still half full, depending on the perspective. Philosophy aside, Kirk hit her with a silent challenge in his gaze.

She downed the frozen drink in one shot, slammed the empty glass onto the table, and stood up. "Well? What are you waiting for?"

CH.15.28
Extreme Dating

All of San Francisco was laid out at Jim Kirk's feet. The view of the city from the top of Mount Davidson was spectacular. It was one thing to see the city as he flew over it in the confines of a shuttle, but that was nothing compared to the unobstructed view from the summit. He could see everything for three-hundred-sixty degrees of perfect vista stretching out around him.

Lynne had taken him to the highest point in the city. Half the trip there was in an old-fashioned cable car. The other half they took the mag-lev monorail. "A little old, and a little new," she'd said. They'd stopped for some sushi midway through the trip, both for nourishment and—as Kirk suspected—to build his anticipation for the main event.

Kirk had enjoyed the cable car more than he'd expected. He didn't have much appreciation for classic vehicles anymore. His stepfather had worn that interest out of him. But experiencing the ride with Lynne had given him a fresh perspective. Watching her excitement at the sound of the clackity-clack of the machinery and the shrill ding of the bells as they rode through the streets filled him with his own joy. And maybe a little something else.

Monica Lynne was a fascinating mixture between a jaded realist and a wishful dreamer. The latter side of her personality hadn't come out much before tonight. And now, she had devised the perfect capper to their evening as they stood at the summit, looking out at the modern city that surrounded them.

The lights on the streets and from the buildings glowed and pulsed, sparkling in the night sky. From their vantage point, they could see all the way out to the darkness of the Pacific Ocean that lay beyond.

She'd picked a good night to take him there. The sky was clear. The breeze was light. They were entirely alone at the top of their world. Kirk draped his arm across her shoulders as they looked down the steep hill before them. "You will now officially be planning all future dates."

She twirled herself out of his embrace. "What makes you think we're going to *have* future dates? That's something you have to earn."

"By beating you to the bottom?"

"You know it." Lynne took off toward the road, running full out.

Kirk was right behind her, the lightweight hoverboard

she'd brought with them tucked carefully beneath his arm. She'd hidden a bag with the hostess at the restaurant. It was a rather large bag and the first big surprise of the night. She didn't reveal the contents—two ultralight hoverboards for street luging, along with the proper pads—until they got to their destination.

Lynne and Kirk reached the crest of the hill at the same time. They slid their boards onto the street and hopped on, lying back only millimeters from the ground. Hoverluge was perfectly safe and legal—on a closed course in the daytime.

On open road at night was another matter.

Kirk didn't care about the danger as the wind whipped past. He looked up at the stars. The street rushed beneath him with increasing speed. He wanted to get lost in those stars, with Lynne beside him, floating on air. But that would be a little too risky. They were coming to the first turn.

Kirk banked right, rolling into the turn. Hoverluge boards didn't have useless things like controls for turning or stopping. It was all done by the fluid motion of the driver's body. Kirk had limited experience with hoverluge; enough to keep him safe. He wasn't so sure it was enough to win a race against Lynne.

Coming out of the first turn, she used the angle to her advantage, picking up speed and pulling ahead. Kirk could only watch as she dusted him. There were few options for picking up speed on the straight-aways.

Luckily the course she'd chosen was full of twists and turns. A series of tight corners followed, giving Kirk the chance to cut the distance between them. It was hard to see on those dark streets. Harder still when they hit a patch that was heavily lined with trees that blocked the light of the rising moon.

Visibility increased dramatically when they reached the residential area and gained streetlamps.

And traffic.

Kirk and Lynne weaved in and around vehicles that were cautiously driving at the speed limit. Their luges traveled considerably faster, whipping past drivers who honked at them as they went.

Lynne let out a joyous whoop. Kirk joined her with his own shout. This was free and exciting. Without the rules and structure of their Academy classes.

The freedom was regrettably short-lived when they heard the police sirens heading in their direction. One of the drivers must have called it in. It was always possible that the officers were heading off to some real emergency. The odds were slim that they were going after a pair of hoverlugers.

The odds got considerably bigger when the police cruisers turned a corner and pulled up behind them. Still, they were going to have to move a lot faster if they wanted to keep up with the speeds Kirk and Lynne were moving.

Lynne let out an expletive as they continued down the steep hill, causing Kirk to laugh. He hadn't been in a good police chase in a while. Of course, that wouldn't look good on their records at the Academy. Kirk didn't much care about that, but he knew Lynne did.

That was probably the only excuse for her going off road and cutting through a private yard.

Kirk banked left at the next available spot, running parallel to her through the yards and neighborhoods of Mount Davidson. He caught glimpses of Lynne with each street they crossed, but didn't see any opportunity to get back in line with her until they reached a road that turned into a cul-de-sac.

They nearly collided when they both went for the single opening between houses. The sirens grew distant, making this a much shorter police chase than the ones he'd been in during his youth.

But the ride wasn't over yet.

Kirk leaned back on the luge, attempting to slow it down so he could safely bring it to a stop. But Lynne kept going. They'd pulled back onto a street, but she clearly wasn't planning on getting off that luge until she was sure the police were a comfortable distance away.

He let up on the board, picking up speed to keep up with her. She wasn't racing now. She was fleeing. With fleeing, there was a certain amount of panic in the way she took the turns without slowing down.

"Monica!" Kirk pushed his luge forward, banking on the turns to bring himself to dangerous speeds. He had to get her to slow down before she did something rash.

Or *more* rash.

Kirk pulled up behind her. "Monica! Stop!"

"No way!" she called back. "You're not going to win that easily."

Kirk had no illusion that she cared about winning anymore. He also didn't think she noticed the impossibly tight turn at the bottom of the hill that ended in a concrete wall.

"Monica!"

Kirk angled his body as best he could to speed up. To find some way to stop her. But Lynne would not be stopped. To make things worse, the sirens were getting louder again.

Kirk could only watch from his luge as she approached the wall at an impossible speed. He had to slow himself or else they'd both hit it.

There was no way she could stop now. But she wasn't even slowing down. She *had* to see the wall. Only a few meters until she hit.

Lynne banked right suddenly. The hoverluge skipped off the curb, sending her into the air. She and the luge went flying higher. Up to the wall. She cleared it by centimeters. The luge was not as lucky. It smashed into concrete.

Kirk wanted to yell her name, but the police sirens

were on the next block. He didn't want to give his location away.

All he could do was lean back onto the luge, dropping his speed and pulling into a skidding stop. It wasn't the recommended way to stop a hoverluge, but it accomplished the goal.

Kirk sprung off the board and ran to the wall. He didn't want to see what it looked like on the other side, but he had to know Monica's fate.

Just as he was about to climb the wall, Lynne's head appeared, peeking over the top. She had a huge grin on her face, and looked none the worse for wear.

"I won," she said.

Kirk wanted to yell at her for being crazy. He wanted to ask her how in the galaxy she survived that. How she made the jump.

But when she leaned over the wall with her face so close to his, all he did was kiss her.

Then they grabbed their boards and got out of there before the cops arrived.

CH.16.28
Investigation Techniques

Spock was sitting in Captain Warde's office when she arrived the following morning with a travel mug in hand. The sweet scent of masala chai accompanied her into the room. She sat behind her desk, placing her PADD down beside her tea.

He had assumed it would be best to start their day by apologizing for his failure at eliciting any information from Cadet Thanas. He had sent her the details of his meeting the prior evening, but had not spoken about it with her in person yet.

Captain Warde did not bother to act like his results had been a surprise. "I suspected as much. I've asked his instructors to keep an eye on him. It could be a coincidence that both of our victims associated with Thanas, but I don't like coincidence. Don't worry about it, Spock."

"I assure you, Captain, I am not worried," Spock said.

The captain smiled. "I understand. What I meant to say was that your report meets my expectations."

Spock suspected that there was some underlying disappointment in that sentence. Possibly an "I told you so" element as well. Not an intentional one, of course. Nothing Captain Warde would ever say directly to him. But Spock was not accustomed to people expecting him to fail at a task.

"Has Cadet Andros regained consciousness?" Spock asked. In light of the lack of evidence, the information she possessed would be the most useful source for shedding light on the events.

"She's still under sedation," Warde replied. "Dr. Griffin felt it best, considering the processes her body will undergo to purge the foreign elements from her system. She should be alert by tomorrow."

"Then we should have our answers in time," Spock noted.

Warde took a sip of her tea. "Don't be so sure. Andros knows that she's going to be expelled. We have a zero tolerance policy on performance enhancement here. It's part of the honor code. There's no wiggle room on this one. So we have nothing to offer her in exchange for the information."

"We could imply that she be included in any charges that we bring upon the doctor that performed the surgery. Those could potentially include murder in light of Cadet Jackson."

She shook her head slowly. "I don't want to victimize the victim. She's already suffering enough. It's possible that

she'll convince herself to tell us the truth, but I'd prefer to focus on other avenues. A lot can happen in twenty-four hours. I'd like to have the case wrapped by the time she can safely be brought around."

"A logical precaution."

"Tell me what you did learn from Thanas," Captain Warde said. "It's possible you missed something."

"Doubtful," Spock said. "But I wrote up a transcript of our conversation for your review. I sent it to you last night."

She tapped the PADD awake. "Yes, I read it when it came in. I'm sure it's an accurate representation of what was said. But I'd like to hear your observations. Much of investigating is not about what is said, but what we can extrapolate from what we see and hear."

Spock could understand the logic behind her question, but he had noted all of his observations in the official report. It seemed unlikely that he could provide any information to expand on his account, but he was not about to shut down any line of inquiry.

"As I noted," he began, "Cadet Thanas was entertaining a female cadet when I came to the door."

"Yes," Warde said. "He does seem to get around."

Spock nodded. "The interruption clearly bothered him, but the ruse of collecting Cadet Jackson's personal belongings was sufficient to get me into the room."

"At which time his lady friend left," Warde said with a

tap on the PADD.

"Precisely." Spock recited his report almost verbatim, growing more unsure of this line of examination with each passing moment. Captain Warde interrupted several times to ask questions about Thanas's responses and demeanor, but nothing that shed any light on the events. Once he wrapped his review, Captain Warde sat in silence for almost a minute.

After another sip of tea, she asked, "What was Cadet Thanas doing when he wasn't helping you pack Jackson's things?"

"Lying in his bed, throwing a tennis ball up into the air."

The captain pursed her lips. "Interesting."

Spock failed to see what was interesting about the action at all, and said as much.

"He was sending you a message," Warde said. "That he didn't care about you enough to give you his attention. Incredibly disrespectful from a cadet."

"True," Spock agreed. He still didn't see the point.

"We've already established that this cadet is particularly obnoxious," she went on. "It could be nothing at all. But sometimes, the guilty tend to react in a way that challenges authority. To come across like they have nothing to hide, 'playing it cool,' so to speak. It's possible that's what he was doing."

"I do not know that we can assume that in hindsight."

"No," she agreed, again with the tone of disappointment in her voice. "But I'll tell you what would have been interesting. I would love to know what he'd have done if you snapped that tennis ball right out of the air." The captain leaned back in her seat, contemplating the possibilities.

She had totally lost Spock with that last comment. He did not understand what Thanas's reaction to an arbitrary action would indicate.

Spock was beginning to feel like he was not the best person to have on this investigation. At the very least, it was clear that he could not function in the manner that Captain Warde most needed him to serve. Spock was left to continue that line of thought while Captain Warde answered a call on her communicator. Her presence was requested at Starfleet Medical.

Warde dismissed Spock as she rose from her chair, and they walked out of her office together. "Admiral Bennett has called a special assembly to announce the news of Cadet Jackson's death. Keep an eye on Thanas's reactions if you can, while the admiral is speaking."

"I am not certain what you want me to look for exactly."

"Well, there's some time before the assembly," she said. "Think it over."

Spock wasn't sure what she meant by that suggestion, but he had an idea of his own. He didn't know that they would have clearance for it, but he suggested the idea to the captain. He would need her permission.

Captain Warde stopped in the hall as they reached the turbo lift. "A practical solution," she said in response to his query. "But I'd like to offer one additional accommodation."

Spock heard her out, surprised that she would allow him to do what she was suggesting, but pleased that the investigation would no longer rest entirely on his shoulders.

CH.17.28
Cloak and Dagger

Uhura spent more time in the observation deck than her quarters. It was an isolated way to live her life, but it was the only way she saw herself getting through the Academy—at least for the next few months. She definitely could not focus when Gaila was around. Her roommate was a complete ball of hormones when guys were in the vicinity. The rest of the campus was filled with distractions as well.

Here she could concentrate solely on her work without letting anything else intrude on her thoughts. Well, *almost* anything.

Karin Andros occupied much of Uhura's thoughts at the moment. They'd never been quite friends, but seeing her convulsing the day before had been scary.

That, naturally, turned her thoughts to Jackson, another acquaintance she never had the chance to know. He was a nice guy. So much nicer than his roommate, Thanas. She'd doubted that he was going to make it through the Academy, but she'd anticipated becoming friends with him. Hearing that he'd died in his sleep like that had been such a shock.

What is it about this incoming class of freshmen? Do we just not cut it?

She took a bite from the breakfast she'd picked up at the mess hall. No more eating on the run for her. She was going to have three square meals a day and make sure her body stayed healthy. She'd just have those meals in the observation deck while she studied.

If she could stop her mind from wandering.

It was the other person in her thoughts that had become the greatest distraction. Would Commander Spock come back? It seemed unlikely once his office was environmentally comfortable again.

She received the answer to that question when the door opened and she found her instructor standing on the threshold. His eyes took the briefest of moments to search the empty room, easily falling on her, the sole occupant. Uhura gave him a shy smile as he entered. She'd expected him to silently take his position on the opposite end of the window ledge, but he crossed the large space, heading straight for her.

Had he come to the observation deck hoping to find me? Why in the world would he be seeking me out? Good thing Vulcans weren't telepathic. Not exactly. They needed to make physical contact to share a person's thoughts. She'd be mortified if he knew how much she hoped that he was there to see her.

He was towering over her before she'd even realized it. "Cadet Uhura, I require your assistance with a delicate matter."

There weren't many other sentences a Vulcan could utter that would pique her interest more. Uhura put her PADD into sleep mode and sat it on the ledge beside her. "You certainly know how to get a girl's attention."

"What I am about to discuss with you cannot be repeated outside this room."

"This is getting a little cloak-and-dagger."

"I do not understand the reference," Spock admitted.

Spock was a refreshing change. Most of the guys Uhura knew were so full of bravado that they'd never admit to not knowing something. They'd just play along with her until they figured out what she was talking about or they moved on to another subject. Spock didn't play those games. She doubted that any Vulcan did, really.

"Cloak-and-dagger," Uhura repeated. "A reference to spy stories about secret meetings and clandestine activities."

"In that case, it is an apt metaphor for what we are about to discuss," Spock said. "I had to receive approval before I could brief you on this matter."

"For someone who doesn't know the meaning of

cloak-and-dagger, you've certainly got the gist of it."
Uhura rose off the ledge so they could be more at eye
level.

Spock suddenly looked uncomfortable. "I regret to
inform you that one of your classmates, Cadet Jackson,
has recently passed."

"I heard," Uhura replied solemnly.

"You have?" Spock said, "the administration is con-
vening a special assembly to announce the news within
the hour."

"Well, it's good they're going to talk about it," she
said. "But everyone knows. You can't keep something like
that quiet. Why would they even try? It sounds like it was
a random thing."

"That has yet to be determined," Spock said. He fell
into the tale of the strange circumstances surrounding
Cadet Jackson's death, segueing into Andros's mysterious
illness the day before. He wove a story that Uhura wouldn't
have believed if she hadn't witnessed part of it herself.

She listened with rapt attention, never imagining that
anyone would go to such extremes to get through the
Academy. Then again, she could understand the stress of
wanting to succeed. She felt that same pressure every day.

Spock detailed his role in the investigation, concluding
with, "My interaction with Thanas was less than satisfac-
tory."

"He's a hard guy to know," Uhura said.

"Yes, but my concern is that if I am to assist Captain Warde in this investigation, I may need to improve my interpersonal skills," Spock said.

"I don't see much need for improvement," Uhura said. She was often annoyed by the human tendency to expect alien beings to change their behavior to fit in on Earth rather than humans changing their expectations of others. Granted, speaking with Spock in class could be a bit intimidating, but it wasn't anything he did intentionally that caused that. It was more the insecurities she brought to the conversation. Insecurities that she didn't feel with most other aliens she'd met. She certainly had no insecurities dealing with Thanas.

"I would prefer not to hinder the investigation any further by creating a divisive atmosphere among the cadets," he said. "And for that, I've been granted permission to request your assistance."

"With the investigation?" Uhura asked. She doubted the administration would want a first-year cadet involved in something this big.

"In part," Spock said. "Captain Warde claimed to be a proponent of what humans term 'thinking outside the box.' What I proposed would certainly fit that category."

"Which is?"

"You possess exceptional communication skills. I would

like your assistance in developing a more casual conversational style," Spock said. "Something that would make my questioning of cadets more productive."

"You want me to teach you how to have a conversation?"

"Before the assembly, if possible," Spock said, as if he were asking her to help him memorize a list of spelling words, as opposed to training him to be . . . *what*? She didn't even know.

"That's less than an hour," Uhura reminded him. "I can't help you with something like that so quickly."

"I have watched you interact with the other students in class," Spock said. "Your ease of conversational skills is something that I hope to acquire. It is a skill that humans excel at. You, in particular."

"Thank you." She was kind of reeling from the admission. She tried not to make a big deal out of either piece of information. To him, she said, "But I can't teach you how to be human in an hour."

"I am already half-human," he explained. "It is only a matter of tapping into whatever skills may have been passed to me through my mother's genes."

"Didn't take you for the nature side of the nature versus nurture debate," she said. "You know, considering how Vulcans are trained to suppress their natural emotions." Uhura hadn't realized that he was only part Vulcan. She'd

never had a reason to question it, really. But still, she knew that he had been raised on Vulcan. Studied Vulcan ways almost exclusively. Far as she could tell, what he was asking was impossible in the time frame he needed it.

"I would appreciate it if we could still make the attempt," he said. "If you are agreeable."

"Oh, I'm fine with it," Uhura assured him. "But I hope there's a Plan B."

"Certainly. Captain Warde has given me permission to invite you into the investigation," Spock said. "I believe she said that I could 'deputize you' onto the team."

"Deputize me?"

"I believe it is an old Earth saying that refers to bringing a civilian into an active role in a police action."

This brought a smile to Uhura's lips. She knew the phrase. She just never thought she'd hear a Vulcan—or a half-Vulcan—say something like that. She didn't need convincing. She'd known since the moment he asked her that she would help him out. But that last part sold her on the idea.

For the next half hour Uhura walked Spock through a basic introduction to small talk. She modeled her discussion on his lecture style of teaching in Interspecies Protocols. Unfortunately, she didn't have as much luck with him as she was having in his class.

"That's not right," Uhura said gently after a third

attempt at small talk. She knew that she didn't have to worry about hurting Spock's feelings, but she couldn't help but be overly polite. He was older than her, far more mature. But in some ways his naivety about human customs was almost childlike in an endearing way.

Of course, Uhura shuddered to think of the mistakes she would make on Vulcan. She certainly knew some humans more prone to emotional outbursts than herself, but she rarely saw the point in hiding her feelings. A few months earlier a bar fight had broken out over her. Sure, that wasn't due to *her* lack of emotional control, but she still felt that she could have handled the situation better.

"I figured out what we're doing wrong," Uhura said. "I'm trying to teach you how to ask the questions. I should be teaching you how to answer them."

"I can see the value in such an approach," Spock said. "Proceed."

Uhura smiled. Dealing with a Vulcan was so much more direct than the games she was used to playing with other guys. "The thing about pumping people for information is that you wind up telling them more than you want to in the hope of getting them to reveal what you want to know."

"An interesting conundrum."

"That's where small talk can be useful," Uhura said. "You need to create a conversation that seems to be about nothing, when it's really about everything. It's all about

lulling your subject into their comfort zone. Especially if the topic is uncomfortable."

"How do I find my subject's comfort zone?" Spock asked. She saw him mentally taking notes of everything she said.

"You let them provide it for you," she said. "Let's do a little role-playing. You're the subject of my investigation. I need to get some information from you without having you realize what I'm after."

"That should make for an interesting lesson," Spock said.

Uhura walked to the doorway, then turned back, pretending as if she'd walked into the room. It was a needless pantomime, but it made her feel more like the part she was playing. "Hello, Spock."

He gave a curt nod. "Cadet Uhura."

"Always so formal. You can call me Nyota when we're not in class."

Spock tilted his head slightly while he selected his response. "Command structure dictates that we refer to ourselves formally while on duty." His performance was a bit wooden, but then again, so were many of his actions. Uhura didn't criticize. She just played along.

"What duty? It's just the two of us," she said. "You know, I don't think I even know your first name."

"I do not use my given name on Earth," Spock said. "It

is unpronounceable to most humans."

She placed a hand on his as it rested on the ledge by the window. "Try me," she said. "I *am* studying Xenolinquistics."

"I would prefer not," he said, slipping his hand out from under hers.

"But I like a challenge," she said. "How else am I supposed to learn?"

"Be that as it may, I find that it makes humans uncomfortable to use it," Spock explained. "They become needlessly embarrassed when they cannot pronounce it."

"Hmmm . . . but *your* mother's human," she pointed out. "Did she use your first name?"

"She could manage it, with difficulty. Usually, she would simply call me Spock," he replied.

"Must have been hard, growing up with a human mother on Vulcan."

"It had certain challenges," Spock replied.

"Is that why you're studying here on Earth?"

"The reasons for my decision to attend Starfleet Academy are complicated. I had been put into a position where I felt obliged to reject my acceptance into the Vulcan Science Academy."

Uhura's eyes lit with interest. "You turned down the Science Academy? I never heard of a Vulcan doing that."

"I was the first."

"Fascinating," she said, letting the word choice sink in.

She'd heard him say that word several times in class. "Your dad was okay with that?"

"He was . . . disappointed with my decision."

She nodded, but didn't say anything.

"Our relationship has been challenged by my actions."

"I'm sure he's proud of your accomplishments here."

"Pride is not a Vulcan trait."

"All parents feel pride," she said. "Even the ones who control their emotions. You can tell."

"I assure you—"

Her hand found his again. "Are you sure you don't want to tell me your name?"

"Positive."

Uhura's lips broke into a grin as her body relaxed, ending their role-playing. "How was that?"

Spock pulled his hand back again. "I fail to see what was accomplished. You did not obtain my name."

"I didn't want your name," she said. "I wanted information on your relationship with your parents. You can't tell me that's something you normally open up to people about."

"That is correct," he said. "But I fail to see how that will assist me in my interview with Thanas."

"No, I don't think you're quite there yet," she said.

"I also noted that you were quite adept at using techniques that would be considered flirtatious," Spock said. "That is not a situation I can replicate with Thanas and expect the same type of results."

"I wasn't being flirty."

"I believe you were," he said. "Touching my hand. The way your eyes locked with mine. The emphasis you placed on certain words. In my time on Earth I have observed those methods of women attracting male suitors."

"That's—That's—I think you've misunderstood." But maybe he hadn't. Had she been flirting with him?

"Perhaps you can employ those techniques in speaking with Thanas," Spock suggested.

"You want *me* to talk to him?"

"I think it is clear that I will not be a suitable interviewer in the necessary time frame." Spock moved toward the door. "We are going to be late to the assembly. Will you assist me in the investigation?"

Uhura joined him by the door. "It could be fun." She placed a hand on his shoulder. "But don't think I've given up on learning your name."

He raised an eyebrow at her touch. She pulled her hand away quickly.

She *was* flirting with him.

CH.18.28
Assembly

"What's this special assembly about?" Kirk asked as he ran into McCoy coming out of the medical building. They fell into step together on the concrete walkway that ran along the perimeter of campus.

"Probably getting around to telling us about Cadet Jackson's death," McCoy replied.

"Ship's kind of sailed on that one," Kirk said. "I figure the only cadets who don't know about him yet are the ones off planet."

"I can think of a few reasons why they might want to get us all in one place to talk about this," McCoy said. "Especially in light of Cadet Andros's situation."

"Is she talking?"

McCoy shook his head. "Still sedated. But I've been doing some research into the problem, and may have found something."

Kirk checked around to make sure no one was in

earshot. The walkway was crowded with cadets heading for the assembly hall, but none of them were close enough to overhear. "Thought you didn't want to talk about this on campus."

"Don't much matter now," McCoy said. "Think they probably want the word to get out."

Something in McCoy's tone warned Kirk that there was even more to the story he'd told the day before. "What have you heard?"

Now McCoy fell into a whisper. Maybe he wasn't ready for everything to get out after all. "Rumors, mostly. 'Bout some clinic in the city that will help cadets get through training. I dug into it last night while you were out on the town."

"Everyone's heard those stories," Kirk replied. "Caffeine injections to help stay awake. Ridiculous vitamin regimes for extra energy. In some cases, steroids. All urban legends. Nothing but lies to tell the incoming cadets, like there's a secret pool at the top of the admin building. None of it's real. The drug screening takes care of all those things."

"This is different," McCoy said. "The kind of thing that screening processes would miss. Like we almost missed the surgery on Jackson."

"What kinds of things?" Kirk asked. "Who's doing it?"

"Still trying to figure it all out," McCoy said.

"Did you tell the captain heading the investigation?"

"Warde?" McCoy said. "Not until I have something concrete. Don't want to go throwing them into some wild goose chase if it *does* turn out to be a rumor. Want to help me look into it?"

Kirk paused before the entered the building. Too many ears inside to overhear them. "Seems that's the administration's job, not ours."

"What cadet is going to talk about this to the administration?"

"There is an honor code," Kirk said. "I've heard some people actually follow it." He didn't have much love for honor codes or excessive rules. Kirk believed in the old school idea of personal freedom, so long as you didn't hurt anyone. But these cadets *were* hurting themselves.

"Not the ones who would consider illegal surgical procedures to cheat their way through the Academy," McCoy said. "Don't think they believe in codes and honor."

"You've got a point," Kirk said. "Still not interested, though. I've got enough trouble trying to keep up with my classes. Don't need to go around solving mysteries to take up my time."

"You mean your time with Cadet Lynne," McCoy said with a mischievous glint in his eye. "How did your date go last night?"

"Ah, Monica." Kirk thought back to the night before. "Let's just say we had so much fun, it was almost criminal."

McCoy smacked him on the arm. "Don't think I need to hear any more."

"Good," Kirk said. "Because I'm not telling."

There really wasn't anything to tell. The truth was that Kirk didn't have much experience in the dating arena. Sure, he had experience with the opposite sex, but "dating" was a whole other thing. He'd never been big on relationships. Or friendships for that matter. Kirk spent a lot of time on his own back home. He wasn't sure that he was ready to share his feelings about Monica with anyone yet—not even with McCoy.

"Speaking of Cadet Lynne," McCoy said. "I mean, *Monica*. Here comes your beloved."

"Knock it off," Kirk replied, as he turned around.

"I get that we need an assembly and all," Lynne said, "but I wish they wouldn't cut into my study time for it. I've got a test this afternoon."

"We think it's about Jackson," Kirk said quickly, so she didn't go on about her studies, considering the subject matter.

"Well, in that case, I guess we should get in there," she replied.

All conversation on several topics ceased as the trio went into the assembly hall. They were early, so it was barely half-filled. Even so, Thanas was waving a hand in their direction. Kirk couldn't figure out why he was trying to get their attention. It wasn't like they were friends.

Kirk ignored him, pointing to the other side of the room. "Plenty of seats over there."

"You really don't like Thanas, do you?" Lynne asked. She and McCoy stood inside the entryway, not yet following Kirk to the seats he'd pointed out.

"It's not that I don't like him," Kirk said. "It's that I don't even care that he exists." If only that were true, but the annoyance Kirk felt toward Thanas took up way more of his thoughts than he wished it would. There was just something about him that set Kirk's nerves on edge.

"Isn't he Cadet Jackson's roommate?" McCoy asked.

Lynne replied with a nod, but Kirk wanted to ask how McCoy knew that. It wasn't like they traveled in the same circles. He guessed that McCoy really had been investigating Jackson's death, beyond listening to rumors on the grapevine.

"Seems like that might be a good place to sit," the doctor said as he moved toward an empty row—and Thanas.

"Why does this guy keep popping up in my life?" Kirk muttered to himself as he reluctantly followed Lynne and McCoy over to the seats. By the time he reached them, McCoy and Thanas had already introduced themselves.

"Didn't expect you to be saving us seats," Lynne said as she took a chair on Thanas's right.

"Wasn't saving seats for all of you," the Andorian replied as his antennae leaned toward Lynne. Kirk bristled.

Somehow the antennae managed to seem lewd. Thanas looked right in Kirk's eyes. "Unless you plan to accept my little challenge."

At first, Kirk didn't have a clue what he was talking about. Then he remembered the comment Thanas had made about something on the Golden Gate Bridge. Some stupid game that, more than likely, would get everyone involved expelled. Kirk let his rolling eyes speak for him as he pushed past Thanas to grab the next seat over.

But McCoy cut Kirk off to claim that chair. He shrugged an "I'm sorry" type of expression, and didn't move. Kirk didn't protest. It would be okay, he thought. He could sit beside Lynne anytime. The farther Kirk was from Thanas, the better.

Kirk was growing increasingly uncomfortable in the assembly hall, which had less to do with the hard seat and more to do with the seating arrangement. He couldn't hear the whispered exchanges between Thanas and Lynne, and that set him on edge.

He knew Lynne had no interest in the Andorian. Kirk wasn't jealous, per se, but he wanted to know what Thanas was saying. He assumed that it was about himself. The few things Kirk did overhear, he didn't like. Every time McCoy tried to engage Thanas in conversation, it made Kirk like the Andorian even less.

Regarding his deceased roommate, Thanas had said,

"Well, he was bound to wash out, anyway."

Of Jackson's death in particular, the response was an even more crass, "Died the way he lived: in his sleep."

But it was the comment about having the single room to himself that sent Kirk over the edge.

"All right," he said. "Time—"

"Excuse me," Cadet Uhura interrupted Kirk's outburst. "Any room for me in here?" Kirk hadn't even noticed her come into the room, but he was just glad that something could shut up Thanas.

Thanas stood, which was more courtesy than Kirk would have ever given him credit for. "Sure, sure," Thanas said as he looked at the group beside him. "Shove down one."

So much for being polite.

"Gladly," Lynne said as she slipped past McCoy and took a seat on the other side of Kirk. He tried not to smile too much at the new seating arrangement. He'd certainly gotten what he wanted out of it. Unfortunately, by the size of the smile on Thanas's face, it seemed like he did too.

* · ⁔ ⋰ ✦ ˙ ✦ · ˙ ·

Uhura had arrived just in time. Admiral Bennett and several senior members of the Academy administration were filing into the room from one of the side entrances down by the lectern. She couldn't be sure if the solemn expressions they wore on their faces were due to the situation at hand or not. They sort of always looked that way.

She'd lucked out by finding Thanas sitting at the end of a partially empty row. Better still that he made space for her beside him. But even better was the fact that she was seated right beside McCoy, who had treated Andros the day before. "Dr. McCoy," she greeted him once she was in her seat. "Any news?"

"Still sedated," McCoy said.

She wanted to press him for more information, but Admiral Bennett called the room to order and got right to the point. "I suspect that many of you have heard the tragic news of yesterday. A member of our ranks has left us, far too young."

There was a mumbling among the usually silent cadets. Word passing from those in the know to those still out of the loop.

"Cadet Jackson was one of our bright young stars."

Uhura's blood boiled when he heard a sarcastic snort from Thanas. Even though she'd never had any interest in the Andorian, that one grunt would have killed any feelings she might have had.

"Cadet Jackson, who was only with us for a short time, had already made his mark in his classes as a standout cadet. We will hold a memorial service for him on Saturday, following morning classes. His family will be holding his funeral at the lunar colony the next day. Those closest to Jackson will be permitted to reserve a spot on the lunar shuttle. I know his parents would appreciate a respectful showing from our cadets, mourning one of their own."

Uhura's head silently nodded along with the admiral's last comment. She would make the journey if she could. She hadn't really had the time to get to know Jackson, but it was the right thing to do.

Then the admiral rose from his chair. His somber expression shifted to one of anger. "The administration is split on my telling you what I am about to say. I, however, believe that it is important not to cover up the truth within these halls."

All eyes were suddenly focused on Admiral Bennett.

"Cadet Jackson's death happened under what we consider suspicious circumstances," he said as a few cadets gasped. "And it was not the only tragic event yesterday. Some of you may have heard of the medical emergency regarding Cadet Karin Andros.

"At this time, we have reason to believe that these two tragedies may be linked. Should anyone have *any* information regarding either cadet's recent activities, they should bring it to me or to Captain Warde." He nodded toward the woman who had just entered the room from a side door. The way she was standing and scanning the room led Uhura to believe something was up. Something Spock hadn't known of when they spoke earlier.

Uhura turned to the back of the room where she saw Spock standing by the door. His eyes had locked with Warde's. Some kind of silent communication passed between the two.

At the front of the room, the admiral continued, "All information will be held in the strictest of confidence."

While the cadets exchanged worried glances, the admiral turned the proceedings over to Captain Halston. Introducing himself as Jackson's advisor, Halston said a few words about his student. It was mostly the generic compliments that one would say about someone they had very little information on. It made sense, since it was only a few months into the year. It only made Uhura feel more guilty for not knowing Jackson better herself.

Captain Halston rose from his chair. "I would like to conclude this assembly with a moment of silence."

The faculty rose, leading the cadets to do the same. Uhura could see that Captain Warde was frustrated that she'd come in at this moment. She seemed to be busting to say something to the admiral.

Uhura also noticed that Captain Warde kept looking at the cadet on her left, Dr. McCoy. Everyone in their row took note of the exact same thing.

CH.19.28
Suspicious Behavior

The cadets were dismissed after the moment of silence ended. Uhura saw that Captain Warde wasn't wasting a moment as she headed straight for the admiral.

Uhura wanted to stick around to see what was up, but Thanas and the others were leaving. This was the best time to get information out of Jackson's roommate, but another opportunity had just presented itself. Something was up with Dr. McCoy. It wouldn't hurt if she ran some quick questions by him first. There was no better way to make a name for herself in the first year than to assist in a high-profile investigation.

It would also be a good way to get Spock to take more notice of her.

She joined the flow of slow-moving students who were making their way out of the room. In the brief moment she'd tried to get Spock's attention to let him know where she was going, she'd gotten separated from the group. She was stuck about a dozen feet behind the people she'd been sitting with, but the crowd between them made it impossible to catch up.

She kept an eye on Jim Kirk since he was at the back of their pack. He'd barely acknowledged her during the assembly. She'd had several run-ins with him since their meeting at that bar in Riverside. Every time he saw her, he made some flirtatious comment or tried to find out her name. She'd never intended that joke to go this far when they'd first met. She figured at the time that she'd never see him again. But now they'd fallen into a pattern, and she wasn't about to be the one to blink. Funny that she was on the other side of this kind of game with Spock and his mysterious Vulcan name.

She suspected that Kirk's sudden lack of interest had to do with his proximity to Monica Lynne. Uhura barely knew the girl, but she liked her enough. She was one of the more serious cadets, and likely to be among her prime competition for graduating at the top of the class. Besides, any girl who could distract a guy away from Uhura was a good one to keep around. She didn't have time for guys right now. If only someone could tell that to Thanas.

And, as if on cue, the Andorian egoist was quick to pounce when she caught up to the group in the hallway. "Miss me?" he asked.

"Not even a little," she said, before realizing that kind

of comment ran counter to her mission to get him to talk. As damage control, she did something she normally wouldn't have done. She grabbed his hand to pull him out of the flow of students exiting the building, still keeping close to Dr. McCoy. "I heard you were packing Jackson's things."

"Well, I haven't really—"

"Need help?"

Thanas nearly stumbled on the walkway. She'd caught him entirely off guard. "You mean you want to come to my quarters?"

She tried not to sigh too loudly. "If that's where his things are, yes."

"Right now? Because I can skip Botany. Seriously. I could use an excuse to miss that class."

Darn. She wanted to go with him, but she had that test. And then a presentation in Astrosciences. Her schedule was full for the day. She'd never get any answers out of him before class. And McCoy was moving farther away.

"After classes," she finally said. "This afternoon. I'll meet you at your room."

Uhura left him with his mouth agape as she hurried to catch up with McCoy and his friends. She couldn't believe she'd just offered to meet Thanas at his quarters. That had been the plan and all, but there was something different between planning to do it and actually agreeing to it.

She hoped she was doing the right thing.

She put those concerns aside as she reached McCoy. "Can I ask you a question? A medical question?"

He looked back to Thanas, who was still gaping after her. "Problem you need diagnosed?"

"Just an unsightly growth," she said with a playful nod toward the guy she'd just left. "But I can remove it on my own."

"No doubt."

"I was just wondering," she said. "Well, I heard Jackson died in his sleep. And, well, I was wondering what could cause that in someone so young. I mean, it's rare, right?" She placed a hand on his arm, remembering back to what Spock had said about her flirting. She meant even less by it now, but she figured it she could use a bit of flirtation to her benefit, then so be it.

But her touch went unnoticed. McCoy was too busy exchanging a suspicious glance with Kirk. Uhura was trying to find a way to ask about the eye contact, but Lynne beat her to it.

"What was that?" Lynne asked.

"What?" Kirk replied, throwing up his hands in mock confusion. If he ever wanted to make it in Starfleet, he was going to have to work on his innocence act. An enemy captain would notice that right away if they were ever in a showdown.

"I think she means that look you two shared," Uhura said. "And don't ask 'what look,' because it couldn't have been more obvious."

"Can you blame me for looking at him?" McCoy joked. "He's just so *dreamy*."

"Very funny," Lynne said. "But neither of you are fooling anyone. Fess up. You know something."

"Would you believe I don't know anything?" Kirk said.

Uhura jumped on the easy set up. "Yes, actually, I would. But it's the good doctor we're talking about."

The group stopped by the fountain near the Academy gardens, where they would not be overheard. It didn't make any difference. McCoy still refused to open up. "I don't know anything," he insisted.

Uhura wasn't the only one not buying it. The doctor wore his emotions on his face. Clearly he wanted to share some information, but he knew better than to do so. This might take some finessing.

Again, Lynne beat her to the punch. "Clearly, you already told Jim what you 'don't know.' Might as well share it now before you force me to get it out of him."

Uhura liked Cadet Lynne more and more with each passing moment. Kirk, however, seemed to enjoy the idea of Lynne forcing information out of him, if the expression on his face was any indication.

After a couple more minutes no one had said anything,

and Kirk finally caved. "Oh, just tell them," he told McCoy. "Word will spread soon enough, anyway." He checked to make sure that no one else was within earshot of the group before admitting, "McCoy assisted on the autopsy."

"Really?" Lynne asked, clearly surprised.

Uhura feigned surprise, since Spock had already told her that much. Of course it was best if no one knew, though. "So you know how Jackson died?" she asked matter-of-factly.

McCoy looked increasingly uncomfortable. "I can't say anything about it."

"Of course you can," Lynne said. "We promise not to tell anyone."

Kirk sighed impatiently as McCoy considered his options. Then looking directly at his friend, Kirk blurted out, "Jackson did something to his body to help him get through his training,"

"Like performance enhancers?" Lynne asked.

"No, that would have been too smart," McCoy said. Since the cat was out of the bag, Uhura guessed he'd decided not to hold back any longer. "Sorry," he said. "Shouldn't speak ill of the dead. But this kid . . . Somebody convinced him that he'd do better at the Academy if he didn't feel any pain."

"I'm not following," Uhura said. Spock hadn't told her the specifics of the surgery Jackson undertook. He'd only said that Jackson had his body altered to help him succeed. "How does someone not feel pain?"

Kirk jumped in again. "Basically, someone shut down his pain receptors."

"It's a little more complicated than that," McCoy said. "But that's the gist of it. Guess he thought that if he didn't feel any pain, he could push his body further."

"That's idiotic," Lynne said. Apparently, she didn't mind speaking ill of the deceased. "I mean, if you're going to do something to help with the training, wouldn't you do something that actually helps, not just mask the problem?"

"It's crazy to do anything to your body just to get into Starfleet," McCoy snapped, his anger growing.

Uhura could practically feel the waves of emotion emanating from him. It was so intense that Uhura felt like she needed to defend her almost-friend. "But Jackson probably didn't—"

"Oh, I don't blame Jackson," McCoy said. "He's just a kid. I blame whoever did this to him. I blame whatever sick, twisted doctor—and I use the term loosely—performed this operation. That person should not only lose his license. He should be strung up by his toes. No. I blame that person."

"I blame Starfleet," Kirk added, stopping the conversation dead.

Uhura was the first to speak. "You . . . what?"

"I blame Starfleet," he repeated. "All their rules and

codes and obsessive training. All of this. It's intense to the point of being ridiculous. Jackson never would have looked for someone to do that to him if this Academy didn't give him a reason to."

All three of the cadets around Kirk started to speak at once, when Captain Warde interrupted. "Excuse us." She stood with a medical officer that McCoy seemed to recognize. This was not going to be good.

"Dr. McCoy," Warde said. "We need to bring you in for more questioning."

"But I already told you everything I knew," McCoy protested.

"Some new evidence has come to light," Warde said. "A few things we could use some enlightenment on." The tone in her voice suggested that she was speaking about more than just some clarifications on the autopsy.

"Dr. Griffin?" McCoy asked.

The older doctor couldn't bring himself to look at his student. "We'll talk about it elsewhere," he said softly.

"But—"

"Come with us, please," Warde commanded.

The officers flanked McCoy and walked him toward the administration building. Kirk and Lynne followed, trying to get information out of the silent officers. Uhura could hear as their voices trailed off in the distance that they were not getting far. It occurred so suddenly that she'd almost convinced herself that it hadn't really happened at all.

She hung back when she saw Spock approaching her. Before she could even ask, he explained what had happened. "Evidence came to light linking Dr. McCoy with the illegal procedure performed on Cadet Jackson."

"I don't buy it," she said, surprising herself as well as Spock for her boldness. "I was just talking to him. The way he reacted . . . I just don't buy it. What's this evidence?"

"That, I am not at liberty to say."

"Look, either I'm a part of this investigation or I'm not," Uhura said, well aware that she was crossing a line. "You want me to talk to Thanas later today, I'm going to need all the information at my disposal. How else will I know if he's telling me something important?"

"I did not realize you would become so invested this quickly."

Uhura tried not to take that as an insult. He was merely stating a fact. And yet it felt like he was calling her emotional in his own Vulcan way. "Of course I'm invested," she said. "I knew Cadet Jackson. McCoy is the one that saved Andros. These people are in my life."

"But you did not really know them, correct?"

He *was* right, but it was also beside the point. "Don't you think it's a little odd that out of all the cadets at Starfleet Medical, McCoy was the one chosen to assist with the autopsy? He didn't volunteer, right? He was assigned the case?" Uhura asked.

"That is correct."

"Wouldn't you say that is a huge coincidence? That the person involved in Cadet Jackson's death just happened to be the one invited to do the autopsy?"

"A valid argument," Spock said. "But how did you know that McCoy was brought in on the autopsy? I did not tell you that earlier."

The words were out of her mouth before she could stop them. "No, McCoy did." Actually, now that she thought on it, Kirk was the one that had told her. But McCoy hadn't denied it.

"Do you not see the fallacy of defending someone who cannot be trusted to keep information such as that classified?"

"He didn't go over every little detail," Uhura relented, knowing it was a weak argument.

"It is possible I was rash by inviting you into this investigation," Spock said. "I did not intend for you to get so involved."

"Well, I am involved," she said. "So tell me. What was this evidence?"

Spock paused while he considered what she was asking. Uhura kept silent as well. She didn't want to push him too hard. Logic would win out. It made sense that she should be an equal partner if they were going to use her to get information. "This cannot go—"

"Any further than me," she finished. "Got it."

"A piece of advanced technology was used in the surgery on Cadet Jackson," he explained. "An instrument so rare that Starfleet Medical only has one of them."

"Let me guess," she said. "That instrument was found in McCoy's quarters."

"No, but it is missing," Spock said. "McCoy signed it out one month ago. About the time that Jackson would have undergone his surgery."

Uhura waited for more. It didn't come.

"That's it?" she asked. "That's the evidence? Maybe he used it for some other reason. Maybe someone faked his signature. He could be getting framed."

"All valid options," Spock said, "which is why he is being questioned. He is not being charged with anything. Not yet, at least."

Uhura didn't like it. The connection seemed flimsy. She worried that the administration was looking for a culprit, and would settle on the first one available. The one that made all the questions stop.

And Uhura was not about to let that happen.

CH.20.28
Unanswered Questions

Kirk stormed into Lynne's quarters, kicking a pair of boots out of his path. The boots slid across the room and under her roommate's bed. Luckily, the girl was out again. It wasn't the best impression to make on her, considering she and Lynne were still getting to know each other.

Probably wasn't a good impression to make on Lynne, either.

"They wouldn't let me talk to him!" Kirk ranted as he paced the room. He needed to move. To do something. *Anything.* "I waited for hours. They kept telling me to go to class. Like I would go to class while Bones is in custody or whatever he's in." He stopped short of kicking another pair of shoes. "Although it would have felt pretty good to pound on Thanas in combat training."

"With that attitude, you're lucky you didn't do anything to get you expelled."

Kirk plopped himself onto Lynne's bed. "Maybe I want

to be expelled. I don't know if this place is right for me. Whatever happened to innocent until proven guilty?"

Lynne joined him on the bed. She started rubbing his neck, returning the favor of the massage he had given her weeks earlier. To Kirk, that seemed like years ago.

"Don't jump to conclusions," she said as her hands kneaded his shoulders. "They probably just wanted to ask him some more questions. It'll turn out to be nothing."

The massage felt good, but it wasn't helping to soothe his mood. He got up again and resumed pacing the room. "If it was nothing, they would have let him go. Do they really think he could have performed that surgery?"

"You don't know that's what they think," she said calmly. "You don't know anything."

Kirk didn't want to hear it. He leaned against the window frame, looking out at the cadets on the quad. He wondered if any of them were involved. If they knew what was going on. "They're probably looking for a scapegoat. Pin it on some first-year cadet and then sweep it under the rug."

"Starfleet wouldn't do that," Lynne insisted. "They want to know the truth. Maybe McCoy knows more than he's letting on. How well do you know the guy, really? How can you be so sure he doesn't?"

"I just do, all right? He wouldn't be involved in something like that. He wouldn't sink that low."

"Maybe he didn't think it was that low," she suggested.

Kirk sat down beside her on the bed again. He figured his nervous energy would have him back on his feet soon enough. At the moment, though, he needed to be close to her—to focus on the slight strawberry scent of her hair, the deep green of her eyes—while he figured out what she was talking about. "You want to explain that?"

"Whatever happened to Jackson was criminal," she said. "Same with Andros. Even if she pulls out of it. She's gone from the Academy for good, no doubt. And who knows what kind of permanent damage she did to her body."

"McCoy wouldn't do that to them."

"You're probably right," Lynne said. "But this underground clinic you talked about earlier. What if they thought they were doing the cadets a favor? Helping them get through this training. What if McCoy was trying to help? He just did the wrong thing."

"But—"

Lynne's hands reached for his, interlocking their fingers together. "Hear me out. I'm not saying McCoy performed the surgery. But maybe he knows something. Maybe he *is* involved, but he's the one trying to make it legit."

"There's nothing legitimate about messing up your body just to pass a class," Kirk said.

"Not the way Jackson or Andros did," Lynne agreed. "But why not some other way? Why not some enhancement that makes someone a little stronger? A little smarter? There are planets in the Federation where people can withstand temperatures that would fry us. Not so long ago on Earth, people could randomly have their bodies pulled and stretched and vacuumed out just for the sake of vanity. Wanting to be the best of the best in Starfleet is, at least, a bit more noble."

"I don't see how," Kirk said. "It's a slippery slope from getting a bit of an edge to trying to create the perfect race through science. They call that eugenics. It's the kind of thing that has caused wars in the past."

She released his hands. Now it was her turn to pace. She circled the room quietly, before finally gathering the courage to say what she was thinking. "Don't be mad, but I don't think you see it, because you joined Starfleet on a whim," she said. "You probably wouldn't have signed up if you had something better to do that day."

"That's not entirely true."

"I know," she said, leaning against the window frame. It was like she was following his path, mimicking his movements. Even when they were upset, they were in sync. "What I mean is that I've dreamed about being in Starfleet my entire life. I took the entrance exam twice, just to see if I could get a better score. I was packed and ready for the shuttle to pick me up for classes a week before it was scheduled. Maybe McCoy, or whoever, thinks that they're doing something good. That they're helping."

"They didn't help Jackson," Kirk reminded her. "Or Andros."

"No," she agreed. "No, they didn't."

"What does any of it matter?" he asked. "All my life I've heard that the Academy is for the best and the brightest. What if you're not the *best*? Not the *brightest*? What if you're just good enough? Does that mean there's no place for you in Starfleet? How good is good enough?"

"I wish I knew," Lynne said.

Kirk remained silent, but he wished the same thing. He'd come to Lynne, hoping that she would say the right thing. Give him the answers. And she had been a help. Just being around her made him feel better. But it didn't solve the problem.

It didn't solve his self-doubt or answer the questions he had about his own ability to make it through. Not that Kirk worried he couldn't excel. He was more concerned with what the Academy might do to him. How it could change him. Was he really Starfleet officer material? Did he want to be?

Kirk needed to clear his head. The day was getting to him. Suddenly, Lynne's quarters felt very small. Like he was trapped in a prison cell, a cell where he would spend the next three or four years of his life. Where he'd only be released to serve time in another prison out in the vast emptiness of space.

Was that what he'd signed up for?

CH.21.28
Clues

The remnants of a young life lay scattered on the desk, half packed in the box that Spock had left behind. Random school supplies, a candle, a framed printout of the Starfleet Academy acceptance letter, and a box of retro candy Uhura remembered from her childhood. That was the sum total of Cadet Jackson's life. At least, as much as anyone would learn of him from the desk in his quarters.

Uhura felt like a snoop going through Jackson's things. He wasn't really even her friend. Their paths had crossed only on a few occasions in the past month. In the library. The mess hall. When she was trying to avoid Thanas. Even though she was doing the thoughtful thing by packing his belongings for his family, she was doing it for the wrong reasons.

"You sure you don't want to take a break?" Thanas asked.

She carefully scooped up the items and placed them

in the box one at a time. "We've been at this for only five minutes." *And you, Thanas, had been whining the whole time.*

Jackson's roommate hadn't packed a single item before Uhura had come to the room, even though Spock had left several boxes behind almost a full day ago. It was no surprise, really. She hadn't expected Thanas to be that generous a person, but she thought he'd at least get Jackson's stuff out of the way so he could claim the entire room for himself.

"I was thinking we could go out for a bit," Thanas suggested. He stood next to an empty box on Jackson's bed. A pile of clothing sat beside it. The clothing hadn't made it *into* the box yet. "Come back and do this later. There's, uh, something going on tonight. Kind of a party. For a select group of cadets. I think you'd have fun."

"I promised I'd get this done tonight."

"We'll get it done." Thanas picked up a few pieces of clothing and dropped them into the box. "I'm tired of looking at Jackson's underwear."

Uhura closed her eyes and breathed deeply. What any women saw in Thanas was beyond her comprehension. She suspected it had a lot to do with the mere fact that he was an alien. They didn't get many Andorians on Earth.

The same could be said of Vulcans. Uhura wondered if that was the reason her mind kept going back to Spock. It was true that he wasn't like any other guy she'd ever met. But was that because of who he was as a person or as a Vulcan?

These were questions for another time. She had more important things to ask Thanas. "I guess you've been getting a lot of questions about Jackson," she ventured, "since you were his roommate and all."

"Yeah," Thanas said with resentment in his voice. "I've suddenly become *very* popular with the faculty. For all the wrong reasons."

She abandoned the desk to help Thanas with the clothing. Once she was beside him, he stopped what he was doing entirely and sat on the bed. Uhura continued putting Jackson's civilian clothes away. "They don't think you know anything, do they?" she asked.

Thanas leaned back on the bed and watched her work. "Who knows what they think? How would I know anything, anyway? We weren't exactly friends."

"Yeah, but you lived in the same room," she reminded him. "I already know more about my roommate than I want to. Guess it's different with guys."

All of Jackson's uniforms went into a separate box. She would let someone else decide where those would go. She wondered if he'd be dressed in uniform for his funeral. Would that be what the family wanted, considering the Academy was a contributing factor in his death?

"Mind if we don't talk about Jackson for a while?" he

asked. "I'm getting a little tired of it. The guy is gone and all. And that's a shame. But everyone keeps asking me about him, like I knew him. We shared a room. A room that we were assigned. I'm tired of everyone coming up to me like we were friends."

"You never seemed to mind attention before."

"When the attention was for things I've done," Thanas spat out. "Not for being the guy with the dead roommate."

Uhura couldn't blame him. She wouldn't have wanted that, either. She moved back to the desk, taking a whiff of the sweet-smelling candy. It reminded her of home.

Thanas got up and moved into her personal space. He didn't quite touch her, but he was close enough to make her uncomfortable. Usually, she'd say something biting and then push him away, but that would run counter to her goal. Instead, she let him put his hands on her shoulders. "Now, I don't mind the attention from the ladies, but everyone else is getting on my nerves."

She couldn't believe he was using the event of Jackson's death to come on to her. *That* pushed her too far. She spun on him, breaking free of his grasp. "What is it with you? Your roommate just died, and you're coming on to me?"

He shrugged her off. "What can I say? I'm socially awkward. It's part of my charm. Would you rather talk about all the other people pumping me for information like you are now?"

"I'm not pumping you for information," Uhura said, perhaps a bit too quickly.

Thanas rolled his eyes. "Oh, please. You've never come to my room before. In fact, you made it perfectly clear that you were *never* going to visit me. Yet here you are. Just one of a steady stream of unexpected guests, like that Captain Warde, the Vulcan, and that doctor."

"What doctor?" she asked. "McCoy?"

"No," he said. "The old guy. That senior officer. The one with a name like one of your planet's mythical creature. Pegasus?"

"Griffin?"

"Yeah, that's him," Thanas said. "Found him in my room the other day before Warde got here to search the place."

"And you didn't tell Captain Warde this?"

"Why would I?" he asked. "Figured the doctor was in on the investigation. Wouldn't Warde already know?"

It was possible that Warde *did* know. But it was equally possible that Uhura had just stumbled upon a major clue. Why would Dr. Griffin need to examine the room? That wasn't his part in the investigation. He wasn't a security officer. Like how Warde wasn't a doctor and didn't conduct the autopsy on the body.

"Look, that party I was telling you about," Thanas said. "It's starting soon. You want to go or not?"

"You go," Uhura said. "I need to finish up here."

"Your loss." Thanas grabbed his uniform jacket and left without another word. Uhura figured that he'd finally written her off as a lost cause.

At least something good came out of this.

She pulled out her communicator and used it to contact Spock. "Meet me at the observation deck," she said. "I think I have some news."

Uhura severed contact, wanting to leave him a little curious. It was a thin lead, but a lead nonetheless. She didn't want him to dismiss it over the comm before she had the chance to make her case.

She took one last look at the framed Academy acceptance letter and then left it in the desk drawer. Uhura figured Jackson's parents didn't need to be reminded of the offer that eventually ended their son's life.

CH.22.28
Golden Gate

Kirk's mind was loaded with random thoughts. He wondered what was going on with McCoy at that moment. What kind of evidence could they have on his friend? How could he help? Was he just overreacting to everything?

But it was the other deeper question that gnawed at him. Would he have said no if someone offered him the chance to take the easy road on his training?

That's what it came down to for Kirk. As bad a decision as it was on Jackson's part, Kirk worried that he would have made a similar one. Well, not exactly a similar one, but where would he draw that line?

Kirk had thought about quitting several times since he started at the Academy. Ever since the race that only had one winner. Where it didn't matter who came in second. It wasn't that he didn't think he could get through. He just wasn't sure he wanted to graduate into a life of Starfleet rules and regulations. What would be the point? To prove himself to a father he would never—could never—meet?

To prove something to himself?

But this was not the time for some pointless exploration of his personal issues. Kirk's friend was in trouble. This was the time to act.

After he'd left Lynne's room he went for a walk off campus, hoping to clear some of those thoughts from his mind. It didn't work. But it did provide focus. With so many questions, what he needed were answers. He was halfway to the marina district when he realized he might know the place to get some.

Kirk doubled back, making his way to the outskirts of the Presidio, where the Golden Gate Bridge stretched across the bay. Thanas had been pushing him since the day before about going to that secret meeting on the bridge. Something to prove who was the better cadet. If Thanas was involved with what was happening, this was the way to find out. And if he wasn't, this was as good a place as any to find out what was going on. If other students went to this mystery clinic, the odds were good they were the type to go for an extreme event like this. Kirk hoped to find out as he stepped onto the pedestrian walkway and made his way across the bridge.

He didn't have to see the small gathering of cadets in the middle of the expanse to know they were there. A section of lighting was mysteriously blacked out. The bridge was lit brightly enough to keep traffic moving smoothly, but the shadows would sufficiently hide any illegal activity.

Kirk strolled up to the gathering, immediately noticing that Thanas stood out from the crowd, acting like he was in charge though Kirk doubted he'd organized it.

"No uniforms, plebe," an upperclassman said upon Kirk's arrival. It was the same cadet that fired the starting phaser for the survival course race. Kirk had since learned his name was Crayton.

Everyone but Kirk was in civilian clothes. He suspected Thanas had purposefully forgotten to mention that detail earlier. Kirk took off his jacket to give himself a freer range of movement for whatever he was about to get himself into. "You want me to strip down?"

"Not necessary," Crayton said.

"Maybe we should take a vote," said a girl whom Kirk didn't know.

Crayton ignored her, focusing on Kirk. "Just remember next time."

Kirk found that "next time" comment interesting. How often did this thing happen? Did Jackson know about it? Andros? "You guys do this often?"

"No questions either, plebe," Crayton barked.

Kirk had enough trouble with authority figures who were actually authority figures. He was having serious problems with this upperclassman acting like he was someone. And the whole "plebe" thing was especially annoying. Still, Kirk didn't expect them all to just open up and admit that they'd gone to some clinic to make themselves better cadets. He was going to have to earn their trust.

That didn't mean he could ask questions. Kirk flashed a smile to the girl who suggested they vote him stripping down. "So what's the deal here? We diving? I thought there was a force field under the bridge to keep jumpers from going over."

"Not diving," Crayton said. He pointed to the tower that was about halfway from where they stood and the mainland. "Think the other way."

Kirk's eyes rose up the suspension cable to the tower two hundred meters above him. It was dark up there with the lights off, but he could still make out the top. Barely. It was quite a climb. "Not very death defying with that force field to catch us."

"It's been disabled," the cadet said. "To make things interesting."

That would do the trick.

"Sounds good," Kirk said. "Do I get to go first?"

"Not so fast," Crayton said. "There's a line. Starts with the cocky Andorian."

"The cocky Andorian gladly gives up his spot for the obnoxious human," Thanas said.

"Guess that's me," Kirk said. "Unless there are other obnoxious humans around here."

Nobody laughed.

"Let's get this over with," Kirk said. The sooner he proved himself, the better chance he'd find out some information. Nobody was going to warm up to him for free, especially not with Thanas there.

Kirk hopped up onto the suspension cable, straddling it while he considered the best way to make his ascent. He knew it was stupid to attempt it without climbing gear, but that was the point. All he had to do was move from cable to cable on his way up, not look down, and he would be fine.

Easier said than done.

Kirk started up the metal orange cable, pulling himself hand over hand. He'd never been scared of heights, but he had also never climbed a bridge before. It was a daunting task. At least the climb wasn't straight up. The suspension cable started out at a low incline, getting steeper the farther up he went. It would be tough at the end, but the starting point was fairly easy.

He wondered if he fell, which would be better: to land on the road with the cars speeding by or to fall smack onto the glassy surface of the bay. It didn't make much difference, really. He'd be just as dead either way.

He was halfway to the tower when he realized just

how stupid agreeing to this was. The climb was getting harder. The metal clasps he grabbed to pull him forward were becoming more difficult to hold onto. There were other ways of getting information. Kirk didn't even know if these people had anything to give.

But he couldn't stop what he was doing. He was only a few minutes from reaching the top. He wasn't about to give up, no matter how dangerous.

The light from a bolt of phaser fire distracted Kirk. He nearly lost his grip on the cable. "What the hell?"

Another bolt of phaser fire struck a meter below him.

"Hey!" he yelled down. Laughter rang out from the bridge. He could barely make out the other cadets in the darkness, but he was pretty sure that Thanas was the one holding the weapon.

Another blast struck above him. Either Thanas was a lousy aim, or he wasn't firing to hit Kirk. Probably his way of making things more interesting. As long as Kirk kept at a steady pace, he should be fine.

Kirk continued to work his way up as random phaser fire lit up around him. The extra light actually made his climb easier, which he suspected was not the point. Didn't matter. He was more than halfway there.

That's when he heard the yelling.

Kirk was surprised that the voices reached him from all the way up there. The wind must be carrying them. He wasn't sure who was arguing, but he was kind of glad that the phaser fire had stopped. Maybe he could make it to the top before it started up again.

He'd only traveled a few more feet when an errant bolt of phaser fire struck above Kirk's hand. It wasn't a direct hit, but close enough. He felt the deadening sensation of being stunned. He clamped onto the cable with his legs, but the reflex of pulling his hand away was enough to jar him loose.

He fell.

Fate had sent him to the waterside of the bridge. Didn't make any difference. At that height, he was already dead.

Kirk braced himself as he dropped the length of the tower.

The vehicles on the bridge continued along their way, unaware that he was about to die. Odd that noticing the traffic flow was going to be one of his last thoughts.

Then he saw Lynne racing toward him. Running at an incredible speed.

A heartbeat later she launched herself off the bridge, latching on to him midair, twirling their bodies so that they were falling feet first.

"What the—!"

Before he could say more, Lynne stunned him with a phaser.

Then the world went black.

CH.23.28
Cold Hard Facts

The shock of the cold water slammed Kirk back into consciousness. It was nothing compared with the surprise of being alive. He fought the reflex to take a breath and swallow a lungful of the San Francisco Bay as he sank deeper into the water. He calmed himself and took stock of the situation. A fall like that was impossible to survive—much less have both of them survive—but he could feel Lynne kicking away from him in the darkness.

He started after her, kicking with the strength returning to his legs, quickly realizing he couldn't tell up from down in the dark. The need for a breath was growing stronger. He forced himself to stop thrashing long enough to allow the natural buoyancy of his body to float him toward the direction of escape. Once he'd figured out where up was, he resumed kicking. But would he run out of air before he made it to the surface?

Kirk pulled against the water with his hands, kicking out

with his legs. He'd survived a fall almost from the top of the Golden Gate Bridge. He wasn't going to let weak lungs do him in.

The last few meters were the toughest, but he soon felt his body break the surface. His lungs burned as he sucked in the fresh air, taking it in with deep, gasping breaths. It took several intakes before he could breathe normally.

"Monica!" he yelled.

"Over here!" she responded. She was only a few meters away. They swam toward each other and embraced, glad to be alive.

"How in the—," Kirk started to ask.

Lynne cut him off. "Later. Save your energy. We've got to swim to shore."

Kirk's muscles strained against the wet clothes that clung to his body. His teeth chattered. His body ached. Suddenly he had even more questions, but none of them were as important as getting to shore.

He kicked off his boots and angled himself toward the shoreline of Baker Beach. It was farther than he'd ever swam in his life, but there was no other option. Having come off just being stunned, he wasn't sure if his struggle was from the water or the residual phaser fire.

Lynne took to the bay like she was born in it, and had to intermittently stop to tread water and wait for him. After a while Kirk told her to swim ahead, not wanting to be the reason she caught hypothermia. She fought him, but he finally convinced her there was no reason they both had to die for his stupidity.

Part of him expected Thanas and the others to report their disappearances. The Academy and local police could have easily had search parties out looking for them mere minutes after they'd hit the water.

The other more logical part of him knew they were on their own. That was the risk of something like climbing the Golden Gate Bridge with people you didn't know. Honor codes weren't adhered to when the activity went against the code from the start.

Kirk swam on. The dark, hulking mass of shoreline grew closer, but he had trouble judging the distance without enough light to guide him. He had nothing but his thoughts for company as he pumped his legs. He didn't want to focus on those thoughts or the questions that came with them.

He didn't have a choice.

Kirk was lucky to be alive. He knew that. To survive a fall from the bridge was unlikely enough. But a fall from near the top of the tower had to be impossible.

Even more incredible than that, he couldn't understand how Lynne had saved him. Shooting him actually made sense. She'd wanted his body to go limp. It was the rest of it that was entirely nuts.

He'd heard stories of people who had survived falls from

bridges before. A tale about some construction worker who dropped a wrench and fell when he reached after it. The wrench hit the water first, breaking the surface. If it hadn't done that, hitting the water would have been like hitting solid ground to the construction worker.

Had Lynne broken the surface for him? If so, why wasn't she dead? She'd put her life in extreme danger to save him. Was she as impetuous as he? Or did she know she had a good chance of making it?

Those last questions rolled over in his mind as he made the final dash for shore. When he reached solid ground, he was too tired to think. He collapsed onto the beach, shivering from the cold, thrilled to be alive, to rest.

He heard sand-muffled footsteps running toward him. "Jim!" Lynne called. He could sense the relief in her voice. She bent down to scoop him into her arms, sharing the little warmth her body generated. It wasn't much, but it was enough.

Kirk rested in her arms for a few minutes, too tired to speak. All he could do was listen to the words of the girl he'd thought he was falling for. "What kind of bonehead stunt was that?" Clearly, her fear outweighed her concern. "You could have died. What were you trying to prove?"

"N-N-Not proving a-a-anything," he said. "F-Finding . . ." He couldn't finish the sentence. He also couldn't ask how she'd recovered so quickly.

"Don't tell me you did this for McCoy," she said. "There are other ways to get information."

Sure, in hindsight that was a reasonable thing to say. Somehow, he hadn't thought that earlier.

"Don't say anything." She pressed herself closer to him. "Just sit for a minute."

He enjoyed the feel of her body against his. Quiet moments like this were missing from what passed for a relationship between them. Their schedules were so busy. Classes so stressful. It was a shame that they needed to almost die to get this time together.

Kirk's body needed to recoup, but his mind did not. It only gave him more of a chance to formulate the questions he didn't want to ask. Even worse, once he was able to speak clearly again, he knew he was putting future moments like this in doubt.

"How did you do that?" he asked. "How did you survive that jump? How did *we* survive?"

"Luck," she said in a most unconvincing tone, and Kirk didn't buy it.

"You knew when you jumped off that bridge that you'd be safe," he said. "Didn't you?"

She shrugged. "Not for sure."

"That was one hell of a risk."

"You could be a bit more grateful, you know. I did save your life."

Lynne was right, of course. But that didn't change the facts. This wasn't the first fall she'd survived. Kirk never asked her what happened after she flew over the concrete wall when they'd been hoverluging. He'd just assumed she'd landed on something soft. Now he wondered if it wasn't what she landed on, but *how* she landed that made the difference.

Kirk kissed her cheek softly. His questions didn't reflect the gratitude he felt but they had to be asked. "I'm sorry. But we both know there's something going on here that you're not telling me. And it's something that could help my friend, so I have to ask."

"You don't think I'm involved with that underground clinic?"

"I think you know about it," he answered. "I think you did something like what Jackson did."

"If I did what Jackson did, we'd both be dead right now," she scoffed.

"Not the same exact thing," he corrected, "but something. You went to that place. You had something done to yourself." Something that could help her survive that fall.

Lynne stared out at the dark water in silence. Kirk knew better than to prod her further. She'd tell him the truth. There were no other options.

He stared out into the darkness with her, squeezing her tighter to his body. Enjoying her warmth. Enjoying her touch.

Their breathing fell into rhythm. Kirk's rapid heartbeat slowed to match hers. They were one in body, but not in mind.

When she took a deep breath, he breathed along with her, knowing she was ready to admit the truth. "In my granddad's journal, the last one he wrote in before graduation, he filled five pages with questions. Just questions. Were his grades good enough? Did he study as hard as he could have? Take the right classes? Train as strongly as he should? There were questions about every decision he made in his four years at the Academy. Those questions were all asking the same thing: Was he good enough?"

"So he had a moment of self-doubt," Kirk said. He understood that. Sure, he might not show it, but he'd had those moments all the time. But then they passed. "It's only natural that he felt that way."

She blew out a sigh. "I never knew if he answered his questions. He didn't write anything in the rest of the journal about it. Or the next journal when he served his first year on a starship before transferring to the deep space mission. He never asked the questions again. Never answered them either. But I could still read the doubt on every page. He beat himself up for the tiniest mistakes. He detailed all his failures and glossed over his successes. It wasn't like he was a screwup, you know. He was actually pretty good at his job, so far as I could tell."

Kirk didn't see how this answered his question, but he

wasn't ready to challenge her on it yet. He knew she would get there.

"But there was always that doubt," she continued. "In himself. And then, when his ship disappeared without explanation . . . I always wondered."

"Wondered what?" Kirk asked. "If it was somehow his fault? That's crazy. There are hundreds of people—"

"Not that," she said in barely a whisper. "Not Granddad, specifically. But what if all those people had the same doubts. What if they all questioned themselves like my granddad? What if that's why they didn't come back?"

"Everyone has doubts," Kirk assured her. "Everyone makes mistakes. You don't know that's why they went missing. A random spatial anomaly could have destroyed the ship before anyone had the time to react. You just don't know."

"But that's why the training is so intense here," she said. "So that we're prepared for anything." She finally looked into his eyes so he could see the fear in them. "That's why I took some precautions to make sure I would always be ready."

"What did you do?" he asked gently.

It was clear that she probably hadn't just desensitized herself to the pain. That would never explain her quick response. Running so fast. Jumping off the bridge at just the right time. Spinning Kirk into the right direction. Hitting the water in just the right way, saving them both.

"Ever heard of gene therapy?" she asked.

"You mean genetic doping?" he said. "Like with athletes? That was outlawed centuries ago."

"It's come a long way since then. My genes have been manipulated to build stronger muscles and give me better endurance. To physically enhance my body to heal faster. To fight off wounds before they happen. It's cutting-edge stuff. And perfectly safe."

"Not for Jackson and Andros."

"No," she said. "I don't know what they did, but it wasn't the same thing. I didn't make their mistake. I researched it. What happened to them isn't going to happen to me."

"It's still illegal," Kirk said. "So there must be a reason."

"Just another dumb rule," she said. "You mentioned eugenics before. That's about the fear of someone trying to create a race of genetically perfect people. This isn't the same thing. This is just a little push. Something extra to enhance what's already there."

Kirk wanted to point out that some rules served a purpose, but he wasn't the person to say that. He'd broken enough of rules in his lifetime. Besides, there was something else more pressing on his mind. "You really didn't know that we'd survive the fall."

She looked down at the sand. "I had hoped."

Kirk wanted to be angry with her. He wanted to yell at her for being so stupid. Not because of the surgery. Because

she nearly gave her own life just to save his worthless butt. But he couldn't bring himself to say any of it.

He couldn't yell at her.

He couldn't ask the question he knew he had to ask.

All he could do was hold her. Hold her and wish that he wasn't about to ruin everything.

CH.24.28
New Leads

"Dr. Griffin, a word if you please." Spock caught the officer as he was exiting the Starfleet Medical building. Captain Warde had suggested that he stage his conversation this way to give her time to search the doctor's office without his knowledge. The last thing she needed was for him to unexpectedly return because he forgot something. Being that the office was Starfleet property, it was well within her legal right to search it, whether or not he was there. Warde preferred to keep things under wraps, in case Spock's conclusions proved to be incorrect. No need to embarrass a member of the faculty.

There was little chance of Spock being wrong. He'd agreed with Uhura's reasoning when she'd spoken with him earlier. Dr. Griffin was in the best position to cover up the events around Jackson's death and Andros's illness. He was the one who had passed along the evidence pointing to McCoy. He also was responsible for insisting that Andros

remain sedated even longer than what some thought was necessary, for her own protection. No one could ignore that the additional delay also kept her from talking.

"Cadet Spock, isn't it?" Dr. Griffin asked.

"Formerly," Spock said. "I am now an instructor at the Academy."

"Oh, congratulations," the doctor said. "Sorry, I didn't know. It's such a large campus."

"Indeed."

"What can I do for you?"

"I am assisting Captain Warde in the investigation into Cadet Jackson's death," Spock said, noticing a sudden hesitation in Griffin's step.

"Oh," Griffin responded casually. "Any new leads?"

"Yes," Spock said. "A potentially valuable one. Almost as useful as the information you provided on that piece of medical equipment that had gone missing."

"I hated turning that file over," Dr. Griffin said. "I really don't think McCoy performed the surgery. I hope you've found something that will prove his innocence."

"Captain Warde is looking into that at this very moment," Spock reported. "In the meantime a question has arisen that I was hoping you could shed some light on."

The doctor walked slower, a little more cautiously. As if he were looking to avoid a physical land mine, while probably expecting a figurative one. "Anything I can do to help the investigation," he said.

Spock stopped them on the walkway. He wanted the doctor's full attention. He wanted to look the doctor in the eyes. "According to Jackson's roommate, shortly after the cadet's death, you visited his quarters. This was between the autopsy and Captain Warde's search of the room, if I am correct. Can you tell me why?"

"I—" The doctor said nothing further as Spock witnessed a variety of emotions playing across his face. Griffin walked over to a bench off the walkway, and sat. "I knew I couldn't count on that Andorian to keep his mouth shut. I should never have stopped by that room, but I've been trying to play catch-up over the past couple days."

Spock was perplexed by the doctor's response. He had anticipated a deflection. A lie contradicting Cadet Thanas or at least some vague excuse covering his actions. This was a much easier conversation than Spock had prepared for.

Before he could press the doctor further, Captain Warde arrived. The security detail that followed her told Spock all that he needed to know. The captain found what she was looking for in his office. Even the doctor had figured that out before she held the cylindrical instrument out to him. It was long, silver, and as thin as a writing instrument.

"Thought it would take you longer to make the

connection," Griffin said, taking hold of the device. "A tri-laser microscalpel. Only one on campus. Funny thing is that this isn't the one that performed the surgery." He looked up at Captain Warde. "I would never do what was done to that boy. You have to believe me."

Captain Warde sat beside him. Spock felt like he should leave, but he knew he had to stay to witness the confession—if that was what was about to take place.

Captain Warde put a hand on Griffin's shoulder. "Tell us what happened."

"I didn't do it," he repeated. "I want to make that perfectly clear. I did not perform that operation on Cadet Jackson. I did not operate on any cadets."

"But you know who did," Warde said. It was a statement. Not a question.

The doctor said, "4F." This earned a nod from Captain Warde, but Spock wasn't sure if that was a code, some kind of location, or something else entirely.

Dr. Griffin went on, explaining the cryptic comment. "That's what they used to call it, you know. Back in the day." He looked up at Spock. "Bet you don't know what I'm talking about, huh?"

"I assume you are about to tell us the identity of your associate."

"I'll get there," he said, turning his attention to Warde. "That's one of the great things about Vulcans. They cut right to the chase. No equivocating."

"Damned annoying about them too," Captain Warde said blithely, as if Spock wasn't standing right beside them.

"That it is," Griffin replied. "Anyway, as I was saying to your young assistant here, '4F' is what they used to call people when they were unfit to serve in the U.S. Armed Forces, if they had some kind of medical condition that kept them from fulfilling their duty. Today it's much more of a clinical term. It's used for those we call 'medically ineligible.' Means the same thing: rejected."

"Actually, it only means that a person cannot serve on active duty on a Starship," Spock corrected him. "There are many other roles in Starfleet that a medically ineligible person can serve."

"Pushing papers," Griffin said, "behind a desk." He looked up to the night sky. "Not up there. Exploring the universe. Making a difference." His eyes fell Earthward. "It was my job to tell the kids who wanted to join up that they didn't cut it. That they were *medically ineligible*. 4F."

Spock failed to see where this story was leading, but Captain Warde identified the issue right away. "What is it?" she asked the doctor. "What do you have, Charles?"

"Inner-ear imbalance," he told them. "Name's not important. What it means is, I can't serve on a starship. Between the artificial gravity and the inertial dampeners . . . Every time a ship goes to warp, I fall down. Not very useful to have a medical officer who can't stay on his feet."

"And there's no cure," Warde guessed.

Griffin let out a bark of laughter. "Oh no, there's a cure. Medicine has advanced pretty far these days. Small bit of a device implanted in the brain. Takes care of the problem fine."

"So what's the issue?"

"It hasn't been tested enough in space," he said. "No guarantee it will work on an extended tour. Can't risk the medical officer going out of commission light-years from home."

Spock failed to understand how that information was relevant to Cadet Jackson's case. "Jackson was not medically ineligible," he noted. "We reviewed his file. Unless you altered it."

"Well, now that's where things took a bit of a turn," Griffin said. "As the saying goes, we started out with the best of intentions."

"We?" Captain Warde asked.

"My partner," he said. "A friend. Back from my Academy days."

"Another medically ineligible candidate?" Spock asked.

"Oh, no," Griffin said. "He was eligible to serve. He left for other reasons. Reasons that should have warned me that getting involved with him would be a bad idea. But he sounded so sincere when I told him what I wanted to do. How I wanted to help the medically ineligible cadets get past the physical. That's all it was at first. Helping them out. With medicine advancing as far as it has, there were so few medically ineligible to begin with. All it took was a matter of adjusting the conditions on the ones we could cure. The ones Starfleet wouldn't normally let us cure."

Once again, Griffin threw a glance in Warde's direction. "So simple, isn't it?" He let out a hollow laugh. "Why should anyone be stopped from joining Starfleet when we have the tools to correct almost any deficiency? When I found those candidates, I'd sent them to the clinic. Promised to get them fixed right up. Made them swear to secrecy and rubber stamp their application."

"How long?" Warde asked. "How long have you been doing this?"

"Five years."

"The first cadets are already serving on starships," Spock noted.

"We're only talking about a handful," Griffin said. "There are only so many cures these days that Starfleet refuses to recognize. Only so many experimental procedures that cadets need to endure. It was supposed to be a limited number of cadets. Only the ones we had the technology to help."

"It didn't stay that way," Warde guessed.

"No. My partner had . . . delusions of grandeur. Wanted

to help the cadets in other ways. Started experimenting. Trying things he never should have. It started with gene therapy. Nothing too dramatic. Never let on what he was doing. Figured if we were going to fix what was wrong with the potential cadets, why not make them a bit better in the process. Then he started seeking out cadets on his own. Ones who didn't need his help but were more than happy to accept it." Dr. Griffin sighed in resignation. "Then he started doing other procedures. Dangerous procedures. In the name of science."

"A name, Charles," Warde prodded gently. "We need a name."

Dr. Griffin looked up at Warde and Spock, and told them everything they needed to know.

CH.25.28
Unofficial Investigation

For the most part, San Francisco didn't have a so-called seedy underbelly. Few cities in the United States did anymore. Poverty had been eradicated on Earth. Crime was almost nonexistent. A person could find a shady neighborhood or a dangerous street, but they were not as common as they used to be.

Kirk had found this one because Lynne had given him directions to it. And he wouldn't have known the level of seediness surrounding him if he hadn't been told. There were no derelict buildings, no sketchy characters roaming the street. It looked no different from the other neighborhoods he'd walked through to get there. But it *was* different. Kirk had been in enough dumps in his life to know when he was in a neighborhood full of them.

The clinic wasn't a dump. Not by the looks of it. If anything, it seemed like a totally respectable operation. Probably was, too. The turbo lift that took him up to the third floor was modern and well serviced. The decor was new. The patients were a diverse mix of people. Most were probably there for innocuous reasons. A few seemed to have questionable motives. Shifty eyes and all.

Kirk was lucky the nurse was able to squeeze him in without an appointment. Luckier still that they had evening hours, though evening had stretched into night long ago. The clinic was a twenty-four hour operation. Lynne had told him that was when the doctor conducted most of his business, when cadets had an easier time slipping off campus unnoticed.

The nurse had been about to turn him away until he'd mentioned that he was a cadet at Starfleet Academy. Probably would have been shown right in if he'd worn his uniform, but he'd gone back to his quarters to shower and change first. Wanted to wash the saltwater of the San Francisco Bay from his skin.

He only waited in the lobby for about a half hour. Several people who had been there before him were still waiting when the nurse came out and announced that Dr. Schaeffer would see him now.

He was shown into an exam room and left on his own. Kirk, alone for the first time since getting there, finally realized how much he was in over his head. He didn't know why he was doing this. He should have just turned over the address to Captain Warde, and let her sort things out. That would have been enough to get McCoy off the hook. But it also would have gotten all the cadets who were involved in trouble.

It would have ended Lynne's Starfleet career.

Kirk considered searching the exam room, but the door opened and Dr. Schaeffer stepped inside and introduced himself. The doctor was on the short side, with a bright smile and a pleasant demeanor. He didn't look like the kind of person responsible for what had been happening at the Academy. He looked like the kind of doctor who gave away lollipops at the end of a visit.

Schaeffer scanned the PADD he carried for the information Kirk had supplied in the waiting room. "So, Cadet . . . Samuels, what brings you here tonight? Forget that Starfleet Academy has one of the foremost medical facilities in the galaxy?"

Kirk forced a smile at the doctor's joke. He was here to play a part. The part of Cadet Samuels, a student desperate enough to play along with the doctor when all Kirk really wanted to do was hurt the man. "Banged up my ankle in a training exercise." Kirk rubbed his hand on the leg that he'd hurt on the survival course. He figured it was best to keep "Samuels's" real reason for being there vague.

"Again," Schaeffer said, "I have to ask why you didn't go to Starfleet Medical."

Kirk looked down on the ground, revealing a shyness

that he didn't possess. "Well, I . . . I didn't want to report it," he said. "You know. I don't want it on my record."

Schaeffer nodded. "The usual reason."

"You get other cadets here?" Kirk asked, as if he didn't know.

"Occasionally," he said. "So, how did you hurt your ankle?"

"Landed the wrong way on a jump."

"And when did this happen?"

"About a month ago."

The doctor reached for his medical tricorder. "A month? That's a long time to go untreated."

"Well, the pain comes and goes," Kirk lied. He'd been fine for a couple weeks. Surely if the fall from the bridge hadn't inflamed the ankle, nothing was going to show up on the tricorder.

Not a problem, really. It was all part of the plan.

The doctor waved the tricorder over the spot Kirk had indicated was hurt. He took his time with it, scanning the leg repeatedly to make sure the readings were accurate. For a brief moment, Kirk worried that he was actually going to find something wrong. He had fallen quite a distance earlier that evening. Even though Lynne had broken the surface of the water before he hit it, there could have been some internal damage.

Dr. Schaeffer returned the tricorder to the counter and

turned to Kirk with a skeptical expression. "Nothing's wrong with your ankle. But you knew that coming in. Didn't you?"

"Nothing's wrong *now*," he replied. "But I did hurt it."

"Possibly," Schaeffer said. "There's evidence of a sprain that healed over fine. Some other fresh bruising to the legs. Nothing serious. Care to tell me why you're really here?"

"You run that thing over the rest of my body, you'll probably find a dozen other old wounds," Kirk said. He figured that would probably be true. His first few months at the Academy had taken a physical toll.

"Maybe you need to toughen up."

Kirk could continue the shy route he suspected Cadet Jackson had used to get what he wanted. He doubted that was the attitude Lynne had adopted. "Look, we both know why I'm here. I need some help with the training."

There was an awkward pause. "I'm afraid we don't prescribe drugs here to get cadets through their tests," the doctor said, playing innocent. Kirk didn't blame him. The proverbial heat, as they say, was on.

"That's not what I mean and you know it," he said. "Word about your clinic has spread. I was hoping for help that was a bit more . . . permanent. The kind that wouldn't show up on a drug screening."

There was a long pause while the doctor considered what Kirk was asking. "Hmm . . . we don't usually get a lot

of unexpected drop-ins."

"You know how word spreads," Kirk said.

"It has lately," the doctor admitted. "Especially in light of recent events."

Kirk went all in. "Yeah, about that. I don't want what Cadets Jackson or Andros had. I want the whole thing. That gene therapy thing."

"What happened to the other cadets was a tragedy," Schaeffer said. "A mistake. I'm not saying that mistake happened here, but the news has reached us. Sad, really, to see such young lives wasted. Of course, what they did to themselves was . . . I doubt it was recommended. But some people are afraid to go all the way."

"I'm not," Kirk said. "I want the full treatment."

"If you'll excuse me"—Dr. Schaeffer moved toward the door—"I need to check some information first."

"Fine by me," Kirk said, leaning back, like he was getting comfortable.

Kirk hopped off the exam table the moment the door closed behind the doctor. He didn't know how long Schaeffer would be gone, but this was a good time to search the exam room. Not that he knew what he was looking for.

He wished there was a lock on the door, but there wasn't. Didn't matter, really. If Schaeffer came back early, it would be just as suspicious that the door was locked than if he walked in on something.

Kirk just had to keep an ear out.

The cabinet drawers were filled with medical instruments that Kirk didn't recognize. He was hoping for something he could bring back to the administration.

He accessed the diagnostic equipment, hoping to find the files he was looking for. Hoping that the doctor kept their records on the individual computers in the exam room. It was a long shot, but worth a try.

The search turned up empty.

The PADD Schaeffer had left behind was equally as useless.

None of this was a surprise. Kirk never expected the doctor to be so lax about the information that could prove he was involved in illegal activities. He doubted that what he needed would even be on the computers that the nurses used.

He had to get into the doctor's private office. That was the only way he was going to take these people down. And the only way he could make sure that he didn't destroy Lynne's Starfleet career at the same time.

● · . ✦ ∴ ✦ · ✦ ·. ·

There was a flurry of activity on the dark San Francisco street a block away from the clinic. The immediate area around Uhura was calm and quiet, but the energy at the command station was palpable. She was lucky to be a part of it. No other cadets were in on what would be the talk of the campus tomorrow.

Starfleet security officers and law enforcement agents intermingled as they planned their move with a quiet precision, under the watchful eye of Captain Warde. She was in unofficial command of the operation since it had been her investigation on campus, but her legal standing only stretched as far as the Academy grounds. Dr. Schaeffer was conducting his illegal clinic on public property. His crimes were a matter for the city of San Francisco.

Spock had explained all that to Uhura on their way over to the staging area. He hadn't wanted her to come along, but she'd been waiting to hear about Dr. Griffin, and grabbed Spock before the security detail left. She wasn't surprised Griffin confessed. It was the right thing to do. Things had already spiraled out of control.

Spock had confirmed that it was much like she'd suspected. Dr. Griffin had been caught in a situation that was not his doing, because he'd teamed with a partner he could not trust. He'd been playing along to avoid being caught while he tried to figure out his next move. Unfortunately for Griffin, the investigation moved just a little faster. Thanks in part to the piece of information Uhura had gotten from Thanas.

"I want in," Uhura said firmly after she pulled Spock

away from the quiet commotion of officers planning the infiltration of the clinic.

"It would be inappropriate to involve a cadet in a security initiative," Spock said.

"Cadets are involved in security initiatives all the time," she reminded him. "It's part of the training. What's your next excuse?"

Spock considered her for a moment. "I find you difficult to debate with."

"You wouldn't be the first person to tell me that."

"At any rate, the decision is not mine," Spock said.

"But Warde will listen to you," she countered.

"That she will," Spock agreed. "But in this instance, I would prefer not to abuse that relationship, since I do not agree that your involvement in this activity is warranted. We have more than enough security and law enforcement personnel as it stands."

Uhura waited, staring him down. She didn't bother to comment on what he'd just said since they both knew one more person wasn't going to tip the balance in any way. She wasn't sure what, exactly, the real reason was, but it wasn't that lame excuse.

The problem with staring down a Vulcan is that it can be difficult to make one uncomfortable enough to force him to speak.

Uhura broke first. "Try again."

She could have sworn she'd seen the barest upturn at the edges of his lips in what some people—not Spock—might even call a smile.

Although they were already distanced enough from the preparations, Spock pulled Uhura farther off to the side to avoid being overheard. "As you already know, the administration is embarrassed by the events surrounding Cadet Jackson's death," he said. "Now that we know a member of the medical faculty is involved, I imagine that the senior officers will be very interested in keeping this unfortunate situation contained. I do not feel that it would be in either of our best interests to bring you into this investigation any further. To put you on their radar, as they say on this planet."

They both looked over to see Captain Warde in a heated, whispered conversation with Admiral Bennett. More than a few glances from the senior officers were thrown in their direction. Spock leaned in closer. "I do not feel it would be . . . prudent."

It was now Uhura's turn to smile, which earned her a raised eyebrow from Spock.

"And you thought you'd never understand personal interactions," she said, answering his silent question.

"All right, then," Warde said, interrupting the discussion. "Time to shut this business down. We go in, access the files, and take every person in the place."

CH.26.28
Undercover

Kirk was back on the exam table when Dr. Schaeffer returned. It looked as if he'd never moved from the spot.

"Cadet," the doctor said in a solemn tone. Kirk didn't need to hear anything more. Not that it mattered. "While I understand your frustration, right now is not the best time for this conversation. I need to consult with my associate, who is, unfortunately, unavailable at the moment. Until such time as I can fully consider your situation, I'm going to prescribe a vitamin regime to help you strengthen up for your training."

Kirk would have laughed in the doctor's face if it wouldn't have blown his cover. A "vitamin regime" was not what cadets were looking for when they came to this clinic for help. Instead, he continued to play his part. "But I really need this. I think you can help me. You *have* to help me."

Dr. Schaeffer backed away from him. "The vitamins will, I'm sure. But that's the best I can do for the time being.

I promise I'll get back to you soon. We have your contact information on file. You have my word, I will be in touch, Cadet Samuels."

"Thank you."

Dr. Schaeffer was waiting for Kirk to get off the exam table. He knew if he went out to the reception area, his mission was a bust. "Can you give me a minute?" he asked. "I wasn't expecting to leave here without . . ." He looked down at the floor.

"Of course," the doctor said. "But if you'll excuse me, I have other patients to tend to."

"Fine," Kirk said. He didn't lift his head until he heard the door open and close again. Then he hopped off the exam table and waited outside the range of the door sensor. Didn't want it to open up while the doctor was still out in the hall. After a thirty count, Kirk took a step into the sensor range and the door opened swiftly.

The hall was empty.

To his left was the waiting room. To his right, more exam rooms and, hopefully, the doctor's private office. Kirk took a step into the hall and turned toward the direction he thought he might find some answers.

All the doors he passed matched the door to the exam room he'd been in. He continued down the hall quickly, not bothering to try any of them. If he reached the end without coming up on one that looked different, he'd systematically work his way backward. The last thing he wanted was to walk in on someone's examination. Considering some of the sketchy characters that had been in the waiting room, it probably wasn't very safe to intrude on someone during a private moment.

The problem solved itself when the last door in the hall was so different from the others that it practically screamed out, "This is the place!"

Kirk hadn't seen many doors like it in his lifetime. It was wooden. Possibly walnut. Stained a deep brown, and appearing quite formidable. He placed his hand on the brass knob. Good thing he'd had some experience with doors like these. Some of his friends back home probably wouldn't know how to open it. Doorknobs went out of fashion long before Kirk's parents we born.

The answers he sought were possibly behind that door. He took a deep breath, turned the knob, and pushed.

It didn't budge.

Locked.

Again, not such a problem for Kirk. His stepfather had a passion for classic antiques. The door to his private study also had a doorknob with a lock. It wasn't the same type of lock as this one, but not different enough that Kirk couldn't figure out how to pick it. He'd become a pro at breaking into his stepfather's inner sanctum. There was never anything interesting there, but Kirk liked the idea of knowing he'd been someplace he wasn't permitted. He hoped to do that again now.

All he needed was the right equipment.

A quick dash back down the hall, and Kirk returned to the exam room he'd been in earlier. The door closed behind him just as a nurse stepped out of a room across the hall. He was lucky she didn't see him. Luckier still that the reception nurse hadn't come looking for him yet.

He probably only had a few minutes. Best not to linger.

A quick search of the cabinet revealed several instruments that could prove useful. He first picked up a metal device about the size of an old pencil. He pressed a button and three tiny lasers formed a pyramid at the top of the tube. No good.

A quick scan of the shelf revealed another slender tube. This one had a tiny metal hook on the end. He shuddered to think what it could be used for in a medical capacity, but it would serve his need perfectly.

With tool in hand, he stepped back toward the door, listening in the hall for silence. The coast seemed clear, so he tripped the sensor and stepped out. His luck held. The return trip was faster than the first. He reached the locked door, inserted the sliver of metal into the lock, and went to work.

It was slower going than his stepfather's study door. Being out of practice and working with a different lock hampered the effort. But within two minutes, he heard the telltale click that signified success.

He gave the knob a turn, and the door opened an inch. He held his breath as he pushed the door all the way open. It would be just his luck to go to all that trouble, only to end up in a supply closet.

The door swung open, activating the lights that illuminated the space. It was the doctor's private office, just as he'd suspected. It was also a total throwback to an earlier time.

Kirk's stepfather would have died had he seen the place. The room looked like it had been lifted right out of the past. It was full of antique furniture, including an old mahogany desk. Leather-bound books lined the shelves. Paintings adorned the wall. And something totally unexpected sat on the desk.

He stepped onto the plush carpeting and moved around the desk to get a good look at the ancient device. It was an early generation computer. Had to be more than two hundred years old.

The computer was in two sections, joined by a hinge in the middle that attached the keyboard to the monitor. It was portable, like a PADD, but considerably more cumbersome. He considered just taking the device, but he didn't want to go walking around with evidence on him.

He tapped a random key to bring the computer to life.

It seemed to be in perfect working order, refurbished to modern specs, but still with its classic design.

Kirk was surprised that the information wasn't encrypted or even that a password wasn't required. He suspected that the doctor thought no one would know how to get past his locked door.

A folder marked "Test Subjects" revealed the computer's secrets to him. It was like Dr. Schaeffer wanted to be found out. Multiple files with more than a dozen cadets' names filled the screen. He hadn't expected so many students to have gone this route.

Cadet Jackson's name was at the top of the list, along with Cadet Andros's. They both had notations next to their names, indicating the procedures they had undergone: nerve reconstruction and altered metabolism.

The rest of the cadets all had the same notation beside their names: gene therapy. Monica Lynne's name was in the middle of that list. Ten other cadets had been through the same procedure. Surprisingly, there was no listing for Thanas. Kirk had been ready to bet money that he was involved somehow.

Now came the difficult part. What to do with the rest of the information?

A quick review of the top two folders revealed that the information in Cadet Jackson's and Cadet Andros's files would be enough to tie the doctor to them. Kirk was no legal expert, but he'd been in enough trouble in his life to know what law enforcement could do with just a little information. Those two files contained more than just a little information.

Kirk attached those files to an e-mail he'd started from Dr. Schaeffer's account and sent them to Captain Warde. Mission accomplished.

Almost.

He next deleted Lynne's file from the computer by dragging it to the trash receptacle icon. That seemed a little too easy to him. There had to be more. It took an additional couple minutes of digging through the computer files to realize another few steps were required to wipe it from the hard drive. Then it was gone for good.

Kirk was about to slip out of the office when the rest of the files caught his eye again. Once Captain Warde received Jackson's and Andros's files, she would put a trace on the communication and follow it back to this office. Then she'd find the other cadet files. Other cadets who had been led astray just as easily as Lynne. They'd be drummed out of the Academy. Their only crime? Wanting too much to fit the Starfleet mold.

Would Starfleet Academy really need the rest of the files? Sure, it would help make a better case against the doctor. Put him away for a longer time. But could Kirk do that at the expense of the other students? Even if

Dr. Schaeffer didn't serve too long, it wasn't like he'd ever be able to practice medicine on Earth ever again. In the end, that would serve the greatest good.

Before he could talk himself out of it, Kirk deleted the rest of the files, leaving the two files he'd forwarded where they were. He'd been in the office too long. He had to get out of there before the nurse came looking for him.

Kirk heard the commotion the moment he opened the door. Law enforcement officials announced themselves out in the reception area. They told everyone not to move. They were storming the clinic.

How did they get here so fast?

Heads popped out from the exam rooms. Faces bore expressions that varied from confusion to fear. Some patients were genuinely surprised that the clinic would be raided. Others almost expected it, as if they lived in anticipation of a daily run-in with the law. Kirk was familiar with that look.

He shut the door. There was no way Starfleet could have received the communiqué he'd sent and gotten over to the office this quickly. Even if they used transporters.

It figured they'd choose to raid the place the night he'd come. He could probably talk his way out of it, but he didn't want to chance it. The last thing he needed was a mark on his record to put him under even more scrutiny.

There was no locking mechanism on this side of the

door. He'd need a key. Even with his skill, he wasn't sure he could lock it with his makeshift pick in time. That would only be a delaying tactic, anyway. Starfleet officers knew how to get through most doors.

A hiding spot was out of the question. They were going to tear this place apart.

That only left the window.

Like everything else in the office, the window opened manually. It took Kirk a moment to find the brass lock and twist it into the unfastened position. He lifted the window and leaned his head out the window.

Three stories up. Not a deadly height, but not a good one, either. He could hear the officers coming down the hall.

• · ∴ ✦ ∴ ✦ · ✦ ·• ·

Spock stood back and let the security officers clear the hall. Captain Warde had detained the doctor in charge, and was questioning him in the first exam room. A variety of other unsavory characters were being led out to reception so the law enforcement officers could determine who was involved and who was simply an innocent bystander.

The old wooden door at the end of the hall drew Spock's attention. The anachronism stood out like a Klaxon in the otherwise modern office suite. The door failed to open when Spock approached. He suspected that the brass device attached midway in height was some kind of mechanism that would allow entrance. He took the metal in hand and gave it a twist, expecting resistance. There was none.

The door opened with a gentle push, revealing a peek into a room from another time. Spock's hand went to the phaser attached at his hip. He removed the weapon from its holster, preparing for whatever could lie beyond that door as he pushed it fully open.

The room was empty save for an expensive collection of antiquities. Spock holstered his phaser and moved to the ancient computing device. He'd learned to work with such an item in his Earth history class. Cadet Jackson's file was conveniently already up on the screen. "How fortuitous," he said to himself. The comment came more out of curiosity than anything.

"What's that?" Captain Warde asked from the doorway as she took in the room. "Whew, check this place out."

"I have found the file on Cadet Jackson," Spock reported as he searched through the computer for more information. "And one on Cadet Andros as well."

"Funny thing," Warde said. "I just got a call from my office. Lieutenant Frango was coordinating the operation from there for me. Seems someone sent those same files only moments ago. The communication trail tied right back to this room. Probably to that very computer."

"Fascinating," Spock said as Warde took over at the computer.

"Did you see anyone exit this room?" Warde asked.

"No," Spock replied, his eyes drifting to the open window. He and Warde shared a curious look. Spock went over to the window. They were on the third floor. A fall from that height would be harmful, but probably not deadly.

The fog rolling in obscured the alley below, making it impossible to see anyone running off into the night.

CH.27.28
The Observation Deck

Uhura was surprisingly awake even though she hadn't slept at all. The infiltration of the clinic wasn't nearly as interesting as she thought it would be, considering she'd been more than a block away from the building when it happened. She really couldn't argue with Spock about not wanting her involved. If this experience had taught her anything, it was that sometimes it was best not to stand out from her peers.

Once everyone who worked at the clinic had been carted off for questioning, there really hadn't been anything to do. Captain Warde had gone off to interrogate the doctor. Spock had to stay with local law enforcement while they took inventory of the clinic, searching for clues.

She'd been pretty much left on her own.

When she got back to her room, she wasn't surprised to find that her roommate was out having a late night. She tried to get some sleep, but the curiosity kept her awake. So many unanswered questions. She hadn't expected Spock to contact her in the middle of the night when he was done with the investigation, but she'd hoped he would.

By sunrise it was clear that her busy mind wasn't going to let her get any rest. She got up, had a good breakfast in the mess hall, then went to the observation deck to study. Well, that wasn't the real reason she'd gone to the observation deck.

She was an hour in to those studies when Spock made his entrance. "I suspected that I might find you here," he said.

She was on her feet in a second. "Commander Spock. Tell me."

Spock ran through the events she'd missed since he left her the night before. He told her about the relative ease with which they secured the clinic. The mysterious arrival of information mere minutes before they found the same files. How they had only found those two files and nothing else. That Dr. Schaeffer admitted to the information they'd found on him, but refused to reveal anything more.

Spock was as succinct as Uhura had expected him to be, conveying every single piece of pertinent information, but he still left her wanting more.

"That's it?" Uhura said. "After all that, you were only able to find two files? Nothing else?"

"Dr. Griffin also named the cadets and officers who they helped alter their medically ineligible status. He maintains that he did not know which cadets were involved with Dr. Schaeffer's more radical experiments. With Griffin's testimony we will be able to prosecute the operator of the clinic," Spock said.

"But more cadets had to be involved in Schaeffer's secret experiments," she insisted. "He needs to go away forever."

"Dr. Schaeffer will serve a significant amount of jail time," Spock assured her. "And both doctors will be stripped of their medical licenses. Griffin will be dishonorably discharged from Starfleet. Neither will be able to commit these crimes again under Federation jurisdiction."

"It's not enough," Uhura said.

"I fail to understand the human fascination with punishment," Spock said. "They will both face rehabilitation for their actions."

Uhura's thoughts turned to Jackson again. The promising cadet he would have been. The possible friend. "It's not enough."

Spock was about to respond, but stopped short when he looked directly into Uhura's eyes. It was odd, but if felt to her like he was seeing her for the first time. Really paying attention to her. He nodded, but didn't say anything more.

Uhura appreciated that he wasn't going to turn this into a philosophical discussion. Whether or not he understood how deeply she felt about this, he clearly respected her emotions. This Vulcan was turning out to be very different from what she'd expected after years of hearing about the cold and unemotional race.

While their eyes remained locked in the silent moment, Uhura thought she saw something else there as well. "What is it?"

"I do not understand the question," Spock said. "I filled you in on all the pertinent information."

She did her best to control the smile wanting to escape. "I can tell by the look on your face that something else is bothering you."

"I assure you that—"

"Nothing's *bothering* you," Uhura finished for him. "Right. But there is something else on your mind."

Now his expression switched to perplexed. Probably not used to someone reading the emotion—and yes, it was emotion—on his face. "No one in the office admitted to sending the file on Cadet Jackson to Captain Warde," Spock said. "One would think they might use that piece as leverage to avoid prosecution for being involved in the clinic."

"Especially since not many people outside the Academy would have even known Captain Warde was in charge of the investigation," Uhura added.

"That thought had also crossed my mind."

"It certainly is a mystery," Uhura said. "But a mystery

for another day. We should celebrate."

"I also fail to see the human preoccupation with celebrating success," Spock said. Again, it looked to Uhura as if he was nearing a smile, but not quite getting all the way there.

"We caught the bad guys. Okay, they might only be getting a weak punishment, but it's something. And, almost as important, this kind of thing is going to look great on our records. That is cause for celebration."

"I see," Spock said. "Unfortunately, unless I'm mistaken, we both have class in less than a half hour."

"Well, at least we can relax for a bit before class." She turned toward the observation window. "You know, this place actually has a nice view when your head's not buried in your studies."

"That it does," Spock agreed.

They both gazed out at the early morning sun lighting the San Francisco Bay. It was the first quiet morning Uhura had had since she arrived at the Academy. She liked that she could share it with Spock.

Of course, there was still one outstanding mystery that she was not about to give up on. She turned to Spock, flashing him a playful smile. "By the way, don't think I've given up on finding out your Vulcan name."

CH.28.28
Endings

McCoy ran the scanner from the medical tricorder over Kirk's lower leg. "No doubt about it," he said. "You busted it up good."

The back of Kirk's leg brushed up against the exam table. He winced at the pain. "Yeah, I guessed that. Can you fix it?"

"Depends." McCoy moved to the table, reaching for the bone regenerator. "Care to tell me how I got out of trouble so fast?"

Kirk shrugged. "Heard something about a raid on some clinic last night. Why are you asking me?"

McCoy eyed him skeptically as he ran the bone regenerator over Kirk's ankle, healing the break. "Just thinking it was awfully fast."

There was a tingling sensation in Kirk's ankle as the bones knit back together. That was it. No pain. Hardly any discomfort. Within seconds the bones were healed. It was as if he'd never hurt himself at all. He stood to test out the ankle. It was fine. "I had nothing to do with it."

That was the truth, actually. He had absolutely nothing to do with the raid. That had been entirely unplanned and totally unexpected. As it turned out, all Kirk had managed to do last night was to protect Lynne and keep the administration from finding out what other misguided cadets had been up to.

That last bit didn't sit too well with Kirk, but none of it did, really. He'd signed on to be part of an organization that forced people to be their best, rejected them when they weren't, and then punished them when they tried to do whatever it took to meet that extraordinary goal.

He'd heard about some cadets being rounded up because they sought unnatural means to overcome their medical ineligibility to join Starfleet. Officers too. They might walk away with a slap on the wrist since the damage was done. It probably depended on the degree of medical quackery Dr. Schaeffer had performed to get them through the physical exam and admitting into the Academy. There was no news on the other cadets, the ones whose files he'd deleted.

"Whatever you did or didn't do," McCoy said as he put away the device, "I just wanted to thank you."

"There's nothing to thank me for," Kirk said as he watched McCoy document the injury in his personnel file. On his permanent record. It seemed such a ridiculous concern at this point.

They made plans to grab dinner that evening, and Kirk walked out of Starfleet Medical with no noticeable limp and no residual pain. Funny how his break was so much less of a problem than his sprain had been. He knew there was a lesson in there about seeking medical attention, but he didn't care to acknowledge it. He'd already had enough lessons over the past twenty-four hours.

Twenty-four hours?

Had it only been last night that he fell off the Golden Gate Bridge?

Life moved fast at Starfleet Academy. So fast that it shouldn't have been a problem that he hadn't seen Lynne since the night before. But it was. She'd avoided his calls when he tried to contact her over the comm. She was ignoring him. That much was clear. But why?

Kirk bypassed the mess hall and went straight for her quarters. The odds were better that she'd be spending lunch there. Away from him.

He was right.

"What are you doing here?" she asked upon seeing him on her doorstep.

He stepped into the room before she could shut him out, not quite sure why he thought that was a possibility. "Hello to you, too."

"Sorry," she said. "Bad morning."

"Have you heard about the clinic being shut down?"

"Why do you think I said it's a bad morning?"

Kirk reached out to her, but she pulled away. "They're not going to find out about you. I destroyed the files."

"All the files?"

"I'm pretty sure."

She didn't look convinced. "And what about Schaeffer? You manage to destroy his memories of me?"

It wasn't like she didn't bear some responsibilities for her actions. Kirk wasn't about to take the blame for what he did. If anything, he'd protected her by destroying her file, along with the files of the other cadets. "Rumor has it he's not talking," Kirk said. "At least that's what McCoy heard."

"Well, that's something," she said. "See how long that lasts. Still, the damage is done. That clinic will never reopen."

"I don't get it," Kirk said. "You already had the surgery. What does it matter if the clinic is there or not?"

"I don't think they were doing a bad thing," she said.

"But Schaeffer led you on," Kirk said. "Made you feel like you needed to do this."

"No, he didn't."

"Look, Monica, I know you think this was the right thing to do, but it wasn't. You don't have to change yourself to succeed here. You're good enough on your own. You've got to stop letting this place mess with your head."

"Starfleet Academy did not mess with my head."

"It made you doubt yourself enough to go to that clinic."

"*No*, it *didn't*," she said.

"Look, I get it," he said. "You're not a victim. But Griffin should never have sent you—"

"Griffin didn't send me anywhere," she said. "I knew about the clinic before I got here. I started the gene therapy before I got here."

"You did?"

"I found out about the clinic on my first tour of the Academy," she said. "A year ago. I was talking to the cadet who gave the tour. Told him how I was afraid I wouldn't get in. How I wasn't going to let anything stop me. He said something weird about knowing how I felt. Well, it wasn't what he said, but how he said it. So I pushed him on it when were away from the group. Next thing I know, he's telling me about this clinic. I went as soon as I could get away.

"Schaeffer had only started doing gene therapy treatments back then. I was one of the first to sign up. He only did minor adjustments to start. A little extra strength. Some extra stamina. Just a few visits over the next several months. Nothing major. Until the weekend after the survival course. I asked him to step up the treatment. I did this to myself. And I don't mind."

"But—"

"Don't," she said, stopping him cold. "Don't try to convince me I'm wrong. Don't try to be a hero. I'm not a damsel. I don't need rescuing. We just see this differently."

"Monica, I think you should go see—"

"And don't suggest therapy," she said. "You know, you can be a little condescending."

He would have argued the point, but he *was* about to suggest she see a therapist. She needed to talk to someone. Someone better than him at making her understand what she was putting herself through was wrong. But he couldn't force her to do it. He couldn't make her see it.

"We just have different opinions," she said. "Maybe too different."

"What's that mean?"

She held out her hand formally. "It was very nice knowing you, James T. Kirk."

Kirk was stunned. He was rarely ever dumped. "What? Why?"

"Because I can't spend all my time here, wondering if or when you're going to turn me in."

"I wouldn't."

"Not on purpose," she interrupted. "You're no snitch. I know that. But things have a way of coming out. You might complain about the rules and regulations. You might rebel in your own little ways. Sure, you might bend those rules. Break them from time to time, even. But in the end, you're a good guy. The white knight who rushes in to save the day. Whether or not it needs saving. You're never going to cross the line. You're exactly the kind of person they want here."

"You are too," he insisted.

"I know," she said. "But in different ways. I'm willing to change to fit in here. You're going to force the Academy to change to fit you."

"Did Dr. Schaeffer give you some kind of sage wisdom along with the gene therapy?"

"You're cute," she said. "But you already know that." She moved to her door, which she opened for him. "I had fun. See you around campus."

There was no point arguing. Kirk saw the determination in her eyes. No matter how little sense she was making, it was perfectly clear to her, and he couldn't dissuade her. Maybe over time she'd see it, but not today.

Kirk stepped out into the hall and said good-bye. It wasn't exactly a teary-eyed, dramatic farewell, since they still had some classes together and were far from out of each other's lives.

But it was final.

As he walked back to his quarters, he had to admit that Lynne had been right about one thing: He wasn't about to let Starfleet Academy change him. There was nothing

plebian about Jim Kirk. Nothing common. He was the best and the brightest, and he was going to make sure Starfleet Academy knew it.

He was also going to be the best on his own terms.